COLOURFUL CREATURES

Dedications:

To Eddy who is the Love of my life.

To Max and Freddie who are the meaning of my life.

To my Mum and Dad who have been a big support in my life.

To Marie-Julie who has bought this novel to life.

COLOURFUL CREATURES

A real woman's tale.

Broken by the betrayal
of friends and lovers.
Her search, not for perfection
but to be whole again.

JULIA LECKEY

Illustrations: Emma & Rose

Special credits & thanks
A big thank you to all the photographers of Unsplashed.
and to Alice Savoie (Cnap) for her font design *Faune*.

This book is a work of fiction, except in the case of historical fact, any resemblance to actual persons, living or dead, is purely coincidental.

Every effort has been made to obtain the necessary permissions with reference to copyright materials, both illustrative and quoted. We apologise for any omissions in this respect and will be pleased to make the appropriate acknowledgement in any future editions.

Julia leckey Publishing
6 Sheridan Road
Wimbledon
SW19 3HP

ISBN
978-1-5272-5055-0

'We are the average of the five people we spend the most time with.'

Jim Rohn

This relates to the law of averages, which is the theory that the results of any given situation will be the average of all outcomes: we are greatly influenced – whether we like it or not – by those closest to us. It affects our way of thinking, our self-esteem, and our decisions. Of course, everyone is their own person, but research shows we are more affected by our environment and those around us than we think.

The Meerkat

Meerkat

From Creaturepedia, the distinctively homemade (but well researched :) encyclopaedia

A Meerkat is inquisitive, naturally curious, mischievous, playful and very determined. They are very social creatures that live in close-knit colonies. They are brave and adventurous, cunning and uninhibited. They can be found in industrial towns like Swansea, or more commonly in the Kalahari Desert in Botswana.

Description
There are few animals on Earth who work as well together as Meerkats; they never stray far from their family even when foraging. They are super cute, with bushy, brown-striped fur, small, pointed faces and large eyes with excellent eyesight surrounded by dark patches to cut the glare from hot desert surfaces.

Warning:
They are constantly threatened by hungry predators, as they are a great-sized snack for Jackals.

M

'The things you are passionate about aren't random,
they are your calling.'

Fabienne Fredrickson

She was not a traditionally beautiful creature.

She had short, wavy hair peppered with blonde highlights. Her brown eyes too big for her face, surrounded by dark patches. A sharp, pointed nose and two capped front teeth that were slightly too wide. She knew that everyone thought the Jackal was out of her league. It was ironic really. She had looked at herself in the mirror every day for the past few months and asked herself the one same question.

'Why do I put up with him?'

Why he was attracted to her she couldn't decide.

Maybe he liked her because she was vivacious and playful, a free spirit with an irrefutable tinge of naughtiness. Her curiosity about life often got her into trouble. She instinctively knew from very early on that, if you are not careful, life can feel like a merry go round. Round and round, with nothing changing. Just the same things, day in and day out. She was determined that her life would never go around in tiny circles, so she painted it very differently to the real world.

Her young, undeveloped mind played tricks on her. She was unsure why everyone around her wasn't more afraid of life. She wondered if they viewed everyone around them as differently as the Colourful Creatures she saw. Was this a form of superpower, she often thought, or just a crazy resolve to save face or hide from the world?

She didn't know.

So she had built up an amazing 'front' over the past year. She was a master of 'the front'. It was nature's way of ultimately protecting herself from intrusion into one's inner self. Outwardly to the world she would stand proud, alert, curious and unafraid, gazing around her, seemingly unfazed. Whereas, inside, she would be needy, shaking, insecure, vulnerable and often despairing. Her mind was an endless, chattering, negative voice. Having an in-depth ability to manage a 'front' meant she rarely showed fear or deep emotion on the outside. But later in life she paid a huge price for holding in her emotions and her lack of honest communication.

'The front' was more of a hindrance than a help.

Jackal

Jackal

From Creaturepedia, the distinctively homemade (but well researched :) encyclopaedia

Jackals are opportunistic, intellectual, ever-vigilant and proficient scavengers. They are predators of small to medium-sized animals and they prey on Meerkats, birds and reptiles.

Description

They are skilful, adaptable and are never one to miss an opportunity. They have a sensitive nose, are extremely curious and can detect the scent of food from 1km away. Many aspects of their lives go unnoticed as they are very solitary creatures.

Warning:

They use their charm to outsmart other animals and trick them with their cunning personality. They have even been known to play dead to attract their prey before catching them with lightning speed.

The Jackal. Her childhood sweetheart. The school head boy. A star football player. A liar.

He would lie even when the truth would do.

He was a slender and upstanding specimen, with a black mantle streaked with a river of silver, caused by a knock to the head when he was young. Very handsome, but extremely sly, he had a propensity to shag anyone that caught his eye. The Meerkat didn't know this to be true at first, for she was only fifteen when they first met. He was cunning and territorial, and she was very much in love. Infatuation, love, lust, first love, she didn't know.

Occasionally she would watch his sexual behaviour from the corner of her eye, but then choose to ignore it. His lust for others she placed to one side. Why did she love him so much? she often thought to herself. Why, because there was always an air of the unexpected around him and when he was with her his intensity and passion would devour her. This lust and affection was as addictive as cocaine.

Beneath the Jackal's heart-warming affection was an undercurrent of control. As the Jackal turned seventeen, he found a new preoccupation with martial arts. With his agile body and fast-thinking mind, he adapted to it with ease and skill. His small bursts of aggression were at first confined to tournaments. But soon he started challenging others while queuing for a bus, waiting for a drink at a bar, or if anyone looked in the Meerkat's direction with a curious eye. When he lost his temper, which was often, it was only, he told her, because he loved her.

'I'm losing your affections,' he'd say with large, melancholy eyes.

'M, do you still love me?' he'd ask.

Him losing his temper wasn't really his fault – but all hers.

Her mother would always worry that one day she would marry him, for she could see her daughter's deep-set infatuation.

But no one could compare to him, so what could she do?

The Bear

From Creaturepedia, the distinctively homemade (but well researched :) encyclopaedia

Bears are anything but predictable. They are magnificent, majestic and mysterious. They are fiercely private and even avoid the company of their own species. They are very protective creatures and are extremely dangerous when they are confronted on their own turf.

Description
They have a keen sense of smell – seven times more powerful than a dog. With their powerful physical presence, they are in love with the wilderness and are the king on land.

Warning:
Hairy, wild and cuddly (especially if it's of the teddy Bear species) made magical and lovable to the world by John Lewis advertising and Disney's *The Jungle Book*. Be careful as everyone loves a bear and they are not as dangerous as everyone once thought.

Bear

'Remember that sometimes not getting what you want is a wonderful stroke of luck.'

Dalai Lama

1

One day, in the Meerkat's first year at college, when reading in a snuggly heap on a train, someone opened the door and strode in. It was an old-fashioned train, still separated into carriages, so they had one compartment all to themselves and this magnificent, monumental being filled up the space. He slumped down into the seat, sniffed the air and looked up at her with a curious gaze. In her surprise, she stumbled and dropped her book on the floor. As they both bent down to quickly pick it up, their heads clashed. The Meerkat squealed in surprise.

'Christ, are you alright?' He grunted. He extended out his large hands to help steady her. The pads on his hands were soft.

"I'm Bear', he said, 'are you sure you're alright?'

The Meerkat sat rubbing her head just above her eye. When the throbbing had eventually faded, she sat back and looked at the curious Bear. Instantly, she was struck by an intensity of desire, overwhelming and intoxicating. She realised then that she knew of him, but had never met him before. So young – so attractive. He was tall, with intelligent, sparkling brown eyes and his sculpted and chiselled face was covered in hair. His hair was so abundant it looked like dense fur. It was unruly and unmanaged. It poked through his buttoned shirt and formed big brown curls on his head. The Meerkat stared, suddenly very alert and very awake. He smiled, his dark eyes crinkling at the corners and beamed back with a reflective glow. It took her a moment to find her voice.

'Um. I'm ok', she chattered. As her head continued to lightly throb, he reached out one of his enormous hands and she gently extended her hand to shake it. As their fingers touched, she felt an odd sensation run through her.

'And you are?' His voice was soft and calm.

'Call me M', she said and smiled.

'I thought so' he said, huffing. Then he made a soft growl in the back of his throat and pulled out a packet of nuts and a book from his bag and sat back in the seat to graze and read. Ignoring her.

She tried to catch his attention: heavy purring, flicking the pages in her book loudly, tutting, applying lipstick, but to no avail. But, his silence and his presence in the carriage filled her with a new optimism. As he strode off the train half an hour later and walked up the platform with a lumbering, ambling gait she was struck by a thought. She could like somebody else. Maybe there was hope for her yet. The next day when she arrived at the station, she looked for him on the train. He was nowhere to be seen.

As the weeks rolled by, the Jackal was less covert with his affections for others. The rumours and sniggering behind her back from her friends grew louder. What could she do? She loved him. In ignorance and love she turned a blind eye; wisdom and experience were not on her side.

'You fool!' they would say when her back was turned. But due to her keen hearing, she heard them. Blushing with shame, she withdrew from the world. This, being far from her gregarious nature, wasn't good for her soul.

Then one day, Bear appeared in her local pub. She spotted his abundance of hair and his intelligent, sparkling brown eyes. Majestic and solitary, he stood at the bar. When she walked over and stood slightly too close to him, he looked at her sideways and sniffed at the air.

'Lavender?' he growled.

She smiled mischievously.

'Alone?' he asked.

'Been stood up' she said, with a fake, exaggerated sigh. 'Fancy a drink?' she asked, with such spontaneity she surprised herself.

Her heart flickered in her throat waiting for a response.

'What about the Jackal?' he huffed.

Her mouth dropped open. 'He doesn't need to know' she said, way too quickly.

'No?' he asked.

'I'm one of many' she replied with a sad smile.

He nodded and smiled into his drink. 'One of many,' he repeated. His eyes lit up with a wicked thought. 'Or the main one of many?' He smiled again, revealing perfect white teeth. 'Or, so I hear', he grumbled.

She stopped breathing and turned to walk away.

'Yes then, a drink would be good' he laughed. His looked up, and he stared appraisingly at her.

From that day he became her escape route. He was mysterious and solitary and never expected too much. The more that she saw of him, the less attached to her sweetheart she became. When he hugged her in his powerful arms, she felt safe. Soon, he became her only means of escape. With his sensitivity, devotion and playfulness he filled up her heart and pushed aside a space that had previously been filled to the brim with her sweetheart. The Jackal never suspected. He was too filled with his own importance and the flock of females vying for his attention. Regardless of this the Jackal knew her new love very well.

For Bear was the Jackal's brother.

'One in one out' her mother would say when she realised the Meerkat had been seeing them both at the same time. Sometimes even on the same day. How right she was. But not in that way. 'A dangerous game.'

The Meerkat's parents and her sister lived in a two-up two-down terraced cottage. It was their safe haven away from the world. Its windows were south facing, which meant it was always slightly too warm. The façade was painted white with a clay-tiled roof, which was green with moss. The house was a happy house. Its dormer windows made it look like it was smiling even from the outside. The closeness she felt to her parents gave her a constant source of joy and worry. They weren't just her parents, they were her best friends and biggest supporters. The thought of them not being in the world one day filled her with a deep-down dread that overwhelmed her. When they would leave this earth, she feared that she would be half the person she was before.

Her only sister was an exact caricature of herself, every feature she had was identical except for slightly wider, or slightly smaller or slightly higher – they could almost have been twins despite their eleven-month age gap. Yet in personality they were opposites. Whereas she was loud, her sister was thoughtful and reserved. The Meerkat would tell the world all her secrets, chattering incessantly, while her sister was quiet and intensely private. But they couldn't have been closer and supported by their selfless parents, they flourished.

Her parents lived and worked in the Salvation Army for many years. This vocation involved endless hours of frugal living: working in soup kitchens, caring for the community and spending hours in the streets, handing out donation envelopes and then collecting them back in the cold, dark winter nights. Street after street, night after night.

Her father was a gifted craftsman who always handmade their presents at Christmas. She would stare in amazement at her gifts, so delicately wrapped by her mother. A work of art. Too beautiful to touch. One year he made her and her sister a miniature dolls' house.

'Open it' her father laughed. He laughed all the time during those years.

'We can always take it back if it's too much?' he teased.

She and her sister looked at the present, breathing in its essence before lifting tiny sections of the wrapping paper between their fingers to unveil what was beneath. They were careful to preserve the beautiful paper for future presents. As if reading their minds, their father shouted:

'Come on girls, we don't need to save the paper!'

Inside the paper was a small house. An identical replica of their own little home. A red door, a white fascia and a mossy roof. When they opened up the front of the house, four rooms and four wooden doll figures looked back at them. Two small girls and two adult figures. Everything inside was a perfect tiny version of their own house. In the lounge, there was a miniature version of their brown coffee table with a bronze fawn and fox, a yellow lamp and soft green velvet sofa. In the kitchen, a large table was surrounded by beautifully handcrafted kitchen units with tiny silver taps over a

white porcelain bowl. One bedroom for her and her sister, with their pink and white spotted wall-paper and white bunk beds. One bedroom for her mum and dad with a large double bed, an ornate oak wardrobe and a rug with a small white dog sitting on it, their dog Ted. Everything was perfectly detailed. Their lives frozen and captured in time. The Meerkat and her sister would spend hours role-playing with the wooden doll figures. The four doll figures became so precious to the Meerkat, she kept them with her at all times.

She'd carry them around in her coat pockets, stroking their little heads with her thumbs.

The time and exceptional love that went into making those gifts made the Meerkat's heart soar. Her father must have spent hours and hours after work crafting and building these gifts in his homemade burrow at the bottom of their garden. The fact that they were too poor to buy these gifts from fancy shops was lost to her in the richness of this selfless act. She felt she was one of the luckiest things alive to have had such devotion and unconditional love. Then one day the little house went missing. She longed for it back so she could play out her childhood again and again. Just the four of them together. But much to her later despair, it was never seen again.

The doll *figures*

Her mother stayed at home until she was eight. The Meerkat never remembered her working when she was younger, except for grooming and adding large rollers to her sisters' hair – of which she had many. Her mum was the youngest of six girls, so there was always one of her sisters laughing and singing in their house. They were her ready-made best friends – what other friends did her mother need when she had five so perfectly made to measure?

Food to her mother was love. She would spend hours in their little kitchen cooking their favourite foods and smiling as she perfected her latest recipe. Her plump little figure was a testament to her own love of food and appetite.

'Come on M, grab the vanilla' she would sing in her Yorkshire accent, 'Get over here and help me cook, I'm making our lavender cake!' – her sister's favourite homemade recipe.

'I'm hopeless!' the Meerkat would say. Her sister was the talented one. Her mum would just laugh and smile, casting her sister a knowing glance. Sometimes a person can smile when feeling only the difficulty of things.

'Let's try again,' She would say. 'Never give up M, you and your sister have a gift'.

The Meerkat's most vivid memory of her mother was when she singing as she baked cakes, though she can't have been doing that throughout the whole of her childhood. One day her mother taught her to sing. Her father sat astride a kitchen chair and hummed the tune. Her dad would eventually become a teacher. He had extended holidays where they would spend hours together as a four, cooking, painting, weaving or building paper models. She had their time in abundance when they were growing up and that time gave her a foundation and happiness that was hard to rock.

In her teens, the Meerkat discovered three things: the Jackal, the Bear and that she had a constant itch. The itch, as annoying as it was, was the easiest to handle. It wasn't one of those physical itches that would have been easy to scratch and forget. No. When she was busy baking, drawing, making, cooking, writing and crafting ideas it seemed to stop the itch that gnawed endlessly at her mind. She would say that her calling was to be creative in some way. As anyone knows who works with creatives, they are delicate beings. It isn't a random passion. It is a calling. She set herself impossibly high standards, was her own worst critic and had a precarious sense of self-worth, and a fragile – if occasionally out of control – ego. The itch made her competitive and ambitious, and when most of her friends found well paid jobs on local factory assembly lines, screwing panels onto cars doors or packaging hampers at Christmas, when she finished her A levels, she wanted more. She wanted to explore her passions. She also needed to escape from the shadow of the Jackal – she'd fallen in love with the Bear.

When one day, after the incident in the nightclub, she could handle it no longer, she looked for a way to escape his claws.

The nightclub episode

The Meerkat, on the Jackal's arm, walked straight past the long queue and into the club. He moved at a fast trot, stopping frequently to examine something, sniff the air or to listen intently. He was ready for any opportunity that might provide some excitement. The locals waiting in line, knowing the Jackal well, never made any complaint and kept their eyes to the floor.

'We should have queued; you always get your own way, don't you?' The Meerkat sighed.

The Jackal looked offended. 'Always', he frowned and then laughed.

They pushed through a long, red velvet curtain and into the night club's thumping music and strobe lights – instantly hammering their senses. The Jackal gave the two, black-suited bouncers a wink when he walked in the door. They winked back. Only inside the club did he release his tight grip on her arm and went to the bar. She stood alone, standing back from the crowds. Within seconds, as expected, he was surrounded by laughing females. Stroking his arms and rubbing his legs. Whilst he was mainly focused on their attention, he kept a closely guarded eye on the Meerkat. She could see his occasional but intense gaze.

Why? She thought to herself for the 100th time. Why do I stay?

His handsome face smiled in her direction and she found herself grateful he'd smiled at her. *Damn, what the hell was she thinking?* She tried to pull her skirt down, it was way too short and the glass of water in her hand was growing heavy.

Then the music changed pace and a heavy drum and base thump vibrated around the club, shaking her water. She held it with both hands. The room felt like it was throbbing. As the music grew louder a light, tentative hand touched her on the shoulder. She recoiled. The hand tapped again. She spun round to see an eager young male keen to gain her attention. With a flick of her eye to the bar, she tried to shoo him away. *Go, go,* go her eyes flicked. But the Jackal had seen.

'Get away from her!' he growled into the surprised face of the male. The lightning speed at which he was at her side astounded them both. The first mistake of the male was to challenge.

'Why mate, she was all alone while you were surrounded by giggling females at the bar. Sorry, I didn't know you were together.' he mumbled.

With a quick rabbit punch to the head, the Jackal knocked him to the ground. The Meerkat scrabbled to help him to his feet as the Jackal jerked back her arm. His second mistake was to laugh in the Jackal's face. The male crawled to stand up smiling and laughing and again got whipped down to the floor. This time he didn't move.

'Jesus M, leave him' the Jackal growled and then smiled and stroked the Meerkat's hair. 'I love you, you know?' he said, tightly gripping her arm.

He said the words 'I love you' with a grimace. Like he didn't quite like the sound of the words in his mouth. That, or he wished he didn't feel love for her, it wasn't really fitting in with his plans. With a flaming intensity in his eyes, he whispered in her ear so no one could hear.

'Remember you're mine, if anyone touched you, I'd kill them.' Then he kissed her hard on the lips with a passion and a force that took her breath away. The females at the bar stopped giggling and stared in shock, eyeing her up and down in surprise. *Who the hell was she?* their eyes asked.

Hours later, when the Meerkat had been surrounded by strangers most of the night, she finally built up enough courage to leave. The Jackal's warning was clear in her ears. The Jackal was nowhere in sight. She crept down the stairs, hidden from view by the crowds. Then, from the corner of her eye, she spotted him. He was leaving the toilets with two giggling girls on his arm and a clear bag, half-filled with white powder, in his hand. She shook her head in disbelief and escaped into the darknes.

The Meerkat had begun to fear for the Bear; this was no longer a game.

When the Meerkat's father and mother stood at the door of their tiny house with tears in their eyes, she felt a flash of guilt. Their youngest Meerkat was leaving home to go to a college in Liverpool to learn how to bake. So early on in her life. They wanted her at home for ever, but the itch and the Jackal would never go away. She wished later she'd stayed in that moment for ever.

'Call every day from the nearest phone-box' her dad said as she left, madly waving. Her mum and sister clung to his side, with tears in their eyes.

'It's only for a summer, nothing will change, I'll be back so soon you won't even notice I'm gone' she had said, as she kissed them all goodbye.

'Fuck off.' the Jackal silently mouthed at her mother's side, standing sentry and stiff. Still angry, she dared to go. The Jackal had brooded and sulked for days. As he bent in to kiss her for the finaltime she whispered 'screw you'. He visibly blanched and stood back in shock. His control had gone. She smiled at his frown, it felt good to be back in control.

Their home town, their habitat, the Jackal, it all felt too small, too confined. A summer-placement had caught her eye and felt like a way to escape from his claws. The Bear she never told. She wasn't sure why, maybe because he was one of the main reasons to stay. But how could they ever be together? This thought filled up her mind intensely day by day.

'I'll see you later,' was all she said as she passionately stroked the Bear's soft furry face and left his bedside on her last night at home. Much to her later regret.

Soon after, everything changed.

Elephant

ElePHANT

From Creaturepedia, the distinctively homemade (but well researched :) encyclopaedia

Elephants have a significant impact on their environments and are considered keystone species. They have an insatiable curiosity and intelligence. They appear to have self-awareness and show empathy for dying or dead individuals of their kind.

Description
They have exceptional brains, and fine senses to intuit danger and opportunities. They have great memories and can remember a location and situation in minute detail many years into the future. They take their time and do everything in life with a measured, graceful pace.

Warning:
They have extreme emotional contagion which is the phenomenon of having one person's emotions and related behaviours directly trigger similar emotions and behaviours in themselves.

Ele

'The elephant keeps walking as the dogs keep barking. The sad fact is that we all have to navigate our way around the dogs in our lives: external critics, competitors, horrible bosses, or friends who undermine. Based on my experiences, I would advise you to prepare for the yapping to increase along with your success or happiness.'

A wise Indian teacher

The Meerkat's home, supposedly for just one long summer, was a room in a red brick, two up, two down Victorian terrace in the middle of an endless row of houses. In her first few days of living there, she would confidently stride up the street and walk straight past the little house. It seemed to shrink back into the endless run, cunningly hiding from her. Only, when she reached the end of the long road, did she often realise her mistake. She'd laugh to herself then and walk back. The house had won yet again.

'Hello? Hello?'

One morning when she woke, she could hear a crashing, stampeding sound rapidly coming up the stairs. Thump, crash, thump. It shook the small house to its foundations.

'Hello? Hello?' The Meerkat in a panic brushed the sleep out of her eyes and realised someone had entered her room and was standing against her window. He looked like an angel filling the room with his presence.

'You were talking in your sleep' he said, panting. The Meerkat shot up, alert and upright and bolted under the quilt. Slowly, she tentatively peered out, his hands opened in a calm, downward gesture.

Only now, when the Meerkat looked properly, she found it

wasn't a man after all. He was a beautiful she. She was captivating. With wide, mournful eyes and silvery, pearly skin. She was dressed in an unusual handmade tie-dyed dress with a large slate velvet coat and was dragging a very large grey trunk across the floor from the landing. The she-not-he shifted from the window, moving with a measured, graceful pace and taking with her the four small wooden figures from the Meerkat's shelf. She stroked each of their faces with her finger with a curious look in her eyes.

'You?' she asked. Holding one of the figures in her hand with a questioning gaze.

'Who are you?' the Meerkat chattered, still frightened by the intrusion.

'Hi', she said. 'I'm your new housemate.'

The Elephant reached out and drew up her grey trunk and sat so close to the Meerkat's bed that she could feel her breath on her face. She exuded so much curiosity and calm. As she moved, her long hair swung around her back and shoulders, in a natural wave-like movement.

'Where are you from?' the Meerkat asked.

'From around the world' the Elephant smiled. Her smile lit up the room. 'India, Tibet, France' she waved her hands in the air as she spoke in a slow, hypnotic movement.

The Meerkat later discovered that the Elephant was actually born in Wakefield in North Yorkshire and had a mixed heritage, which included Portuguese, Burmese and Indian. Her Anglo-Indian parents were so overprotective that she had very little freedom. They followed her round and even though they were very nurturing and protective they were also stifling. As soon as she was eighteen, she applied to nursing school enough miles away from her parents to give her some space. Inbetween studying to be a nurse she was training to be enlightened. Spiritual enlightenment in the Western world had taken on a romantic meaning, and the Elephant wanted to embrace its qualities of self-realisation and find her true self. Whatever that meant.

The Meerkat had enrolled at a nearby college famous for their baking courses. She needed some space, and where better to find that than whilst baking. Her favourite pastime. Within hours she was thrilled to be away from the claws of the Jackal. She hoped maybe he would forget her and she could finally be with the Bear.

Over the next few days, while the Meerkat was taking her baking-classes at the nearby college, she grew to love the Elephant. With the Elephant's sad eyes you could be forgiven for thinking she was melancholy – but she was, in fact, a natural leader, gentle, playful and reliable. The Elephant had an insatiable curiosity and a far-reaching emotional intelligence. The Meerkat soon realised that due to the Elephant's emotional traits she would subconsciously mirror the Meerkat's expressions and emotions. Whenever the Meerkat told the Elephant stories of her past, she would laugh or cry depending on the subject. As unusual as it was for the Meerkat to understand this behaviour, it fostered a deep emotional synchrony between them. A depth of friendship she'd never experienced before – a real soul mate.

With the Elephant's imposing physical presence and kind, spiritual demeanour, she seemed to move quickly through life. Few barriers held her back. The Elephant loved basking in mud baths and shouting stories to the Meerkat. She wanted to share her latest theory of life. No shame of her nakedness. Every story she delivered with such conviction.

'You know M', she said, 'I've lived many lives. I've been reincarnated many times you know.'

'Really?' the Meerkat giggled. She had just cooked herself a

The Elephant loved basking in mud baths

tasty chicken sandwich and was sitting alert and upright on the edge of the bath, nibbling at its crust.

'One of the lives I remember, was living in China during the revolution. I married a Chinese man who repeatedly beat and strangled me'. She casually stretched out her toe and pushed it up under the tap.

'Oh God, that sounds awful.' the Meerkat said.

'In the end', the Elephant said, 'He strangled me to death when I was pregnant with our first child'.

The Elephant wrapped her hands around her neck to emphasise the neck-hold and added a twisting gesture to make sure the Meerkat fully understood. The Meerkat flashed her a worried look. She wasn't sure if it was coincidental, but each of the Elephant's past lives had a similar ending with her being strangled, beaten or raped. This wasn't the first time she'd heard this story.

'Come on M', Ele said. 'You've got to believe in reincarnation, do you know what it is?

'It seems too far-fetched' the Meerkat frowned.

'It's when the mind or essence of a being is reborn into a new body' the Elephant said 'When you think about it, everyone has been your mum, dad, son, daughter and lunch in their previous lives on earth', she laughed. 'Yes, your lunch!' she said.

'What?' The Meerkat asked.

'You could be eating your son from a previous life for your lunch right now', the Elephant laughed again, looking at the Meerkat's frowning face. 'Because he has had the ill-fortune to be born into this life as a chicken'. She dipped her head under the water and rubbed at her face.

A sandwich wedged full of hot chicken

The Meerkat sniffed at her sandwich, wedged full of hot chicken, and suddenly lost her appetite.

'Thanks.' the Meerkat said, as she threw the half-eaten sandwich into the bin. At times when the Elephant's theories were expressed the Meerkat merely nodded in agreement, but deep down she had started to worry about the Elephant's sanity.

Soon after that, the Meerkat's sister died.

From that moment on, the Elephant never left her side. The four wooden doll figures were quickly moved from her shelf into the trunk and for a while, the Meerkat worried about her own sanity.

The Crab

Crab

From Creaturepedia, the distinctively homemade (but well researched :) encyclopaedia

Crabs are generally covered with tough armour and formidable claws. The crab is one of the oldest and hardest of all nature's beings. It has a tough side and a very soft side. Not only does it have a soft inside that's good to eat but a hard side that's not good to eat and difficult to crack.

Description

Has unusual endurance.

Adventurous, territorial, quick, cunning and in general a loner. It changes its home seventeen times in a lifetime to help it survive and grow.

Warning:

A survivor of ice ages, dinosaurs and asteroids. A survivor at all costs.

'The secret of change is to focus all of your energy, not on fighting the old but on building the new.'

Dan Millman

What did she regret most in life, meeting the Crab or the ways things turned out?

It was an exceptionally warm day in October, and the Meerkat was waiting for an interview. She didn't want to go home. She needed a job. Round and round in tiny circles, on the brink of despair. She'd been in endless, heart-wrenching interviews with the police and no one was any closer to knowing who killed her sister.

The Crab, never one to blend in, marched over and stood in the main entrance to the restaurant wearing an extravagant long red leather coat, a black furry hat and a tight, red, all-in-one jumpsuit. She had naturally, stunning bright red hair and piercing black eyes. A sharp, firm nose and plump, blossoming lips that she constantly licked, with a quick flick of her tongue, to ensure they always stayed moist. As the Crab marched past her on that bright, sunny day, she gave her a sideways look. Her eyes were friendly, smiling and hopeful.

'Are you waiting for an interview, are you a friend of the owner?' she asked.

'Yes', said the Meerkat sullenly. Neither said anything for a minute.

The Meerkat could feel the Crab's many eyes fixed intently on her. The Meerkat took a gulp of her tea.

'How about another drink? How about a nice brandy?' the Crab asked and shuffled on the steps.

'Why not?' The Meerkat sighed.

It was midnight when the Meerkat got home – she was rotten drunk. The Meerkat had even laughed once. The Crab had offered to drop her off in a taxi, she said she wanted to see where she lived. But it was more as the Meerkat later suspected that the Crab didn't believe she'd make it home on her own. She could feel the Elephant and the Crab glaring at each other as she threw up over their neighbour's wall into their garden. She watched their red roses shrivel with the acidic sick of the brandy. The Elephant then pulled her inside and gently showered her down whilst she sobbed in despair into her hands.

'I can't live like this E, I can't live like this!' the Meerkat repeated over and over again. The sick smell was clinging to her hair and she could smell the rancid scent of the brandy.

'You can and you will', the Elephant said as she helped her into bed and lay next to her stroking her hair. The sobs wrenched at the Meerkat's body, threatening to burst her heart. 'You've got no bloody choice M, life can be shit like this.'

The next morning, as the Meerkat left the house, her neighbour stood fuming, inspecting her shrivelled roses.

'Kindly stand in our garden and throw up in your own garden next time!' she croaked.

Within a month, the Crab had moved into the little house and was sleeping in the attic. While their natures and personalities were never supposed to work together, they somehow did. By then, the Meerkat and the Crab shared nearly all of their time, their lives and their friends. Their relationship became as intertwined as any young couple in love. An odd combination of nature.

'Why do you love the Crab?' the Elephant asked her one day, her eyes growing with amazement.

The Meerkat shuffled and her brow creased. 'I find her so...' the Elephant said, '...so incredibly difficult to love, she's so hard and indifferent to the world, she doesn't seem to give a shit about anyone'.

The question made the Meerkat pause. Her feelings for the Crab were somehow tricky to articulate. It was like an elaborate mind game that played out time and time again.

'When we are together', the Meerkat tried to explain, 'the Crab brings out a side in me which I thought had died' she said. 'It used to exist, but I lost it.' she sighed. 'But now, it's like a new chapter has started. I'm moving forward again – she won't let me be sad, do you understand that?' she strained to articulate the thoughts in her mind.

'I worry for you, M' the Elephant said. 'You sound like you have it all worked out, but she's not right you know, life is one big joke to her and she doesn't care as long as the world makes her laugh.' The Elephant fell into a profound silence and wouldn't speak again on the subject.

The Crab's personality and character filled the Meerkat's life again with a new energy. With the Crab, there was no over-analysing or self-doubt, just a real force of nature that the Meerkat envied. Did that mean that when she was with the Crab, she was at her most moral or kind? She often weighed this up. *No*. It was her, but her with a sense of nothing to lose. Her, living in the now, as wildly and passionately as she possibly could. The Crab's personality and character filled her life with a new passion. Anything and everything was possible again. Yet everything at the same time was so delicately balanced on a fine, sharp raw edge. The Crab had the power and energy to change the atmosphere in any room in seconds. From a blazing row to an intense sense of fun and laughter. From a place of laughter and joy into a vast space of conflict.

The Crab had such an unusual, seductive charm. A favoured delicacy that everyone wanted to devour. They fell in love with her dominating sexual nature, mistaking her passion and lust for love.

Eventually and inevitably she always ended up devouring them. Which resulted in endless streams of full-grown crying males appearing on their doorstep broken, wondering why the Crab had cast them aside when only the day before she had seemed so deeply in love. The Crab would laugh at their naivety and relate back to the Meerkat a new sexual position or game that she had learnt. She was always amazed that they had mistaken her attention for love. One of the most vivid nights was the night the Crab met the ginger Tomcat. They had been invited to an erotic, shimmering and pulsating gathering.

The Elephant had point blank refused to come.

Individuals wearing only flashes of exotic furs and feathers to cover their nakedness wandered around the room looking for adventure. As they entered the party, the Meerkat felt suddenly small and clumsy. She hadn't known quite what to wear, and her old sandy dress felt out of place. The Crab made a glamorous marching entrance behind her, flashing her elegant, slick fitted red attire, dominating the room with her presence. The Crab captivated all eyes in the place. The Meerkat thought she glowed that night as she glided quickly across the floor. There was no escaping her gaze.

The Crab eyed the room for prey. A large, ginger Tomcat moved too quickly and caught her attention. The Tomcat, believing he was the superior species, didn't realise the trap he was about to fall into. The Tomcat, even though he was still very young, had started to go bald. Tiny ginger sprigs of hair sat alongside his shiny bald patches. In a room, he didn't stand out because of his looks, but more because of his extreme height and bulky physique. He had a freckled face that was unattractive and fierce, which perfectly complemented his dark moods. But the main thing that the Meerkat remembered about Tom was when he sat and wailed on their doorstep like a baby when the Crab ended their turbulent relationship.

'Please come down and let me in!' Tom howled 'I love you, I can't do without you in my life!' he then whined into his hands.

'GO AWAY, ITS OVER!' the Crab screamed from the window.

The Meerkat then heard her scurrying around in the attic, looking for something. She appeared at the window with a bottle in her hand. She emptied the bottle of red wine over his head. It splattered down his furry coat and face, covering him all over in the red, sticky liquid.

'But I love you!' wailed the Tomcat at high volume in utter disbelief. His brown eyes looked melancholy and tearful.

'Shall we let him in?' the Meerkat whispered from the hall. 'He's crying, I feel awful for him, we can help him clean up.'

To make sure they all got the message that the relationship was over, the Crab made careful aim with a second bottle and threw it hard against the wall at the end of their garden. It hit their neighbour's prize greenhouse and exploded, red

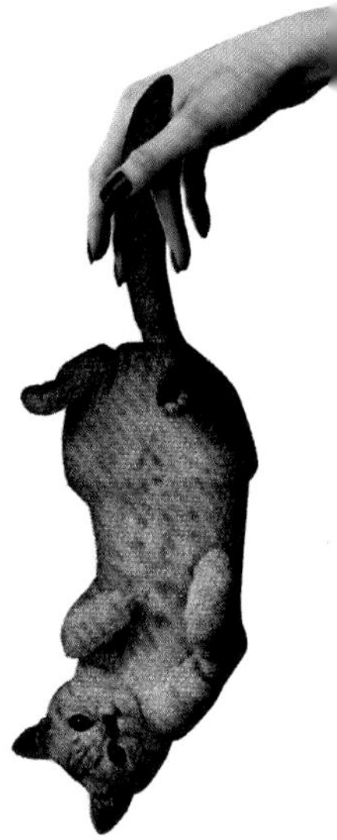

wine dripped down its glass like it was bleeding. Their poor neighbour, standing inside gently tending to his roses, fell to the floor and wrapped his hands round his ears like a bomb had gone off. The sound of the smash echoed around the whole house and in his shock and surprise the Tom scampered away into the night.

'KEEP OUT M, it's over.' the Crab snapped at her.

Loud banging at their door five minutes later by their neighbour was ignored. They all hid in the bedroom.

'NEXT TIME', he shouted through the letter box, 'THROW A BOTTLE AT YOUR OWN GREENHOUSE YOU MAD CREATURES!'

The Crab had kept the Tom close for months because she'd grown addicted to his fondness for sex with a bottle. The bottle became a sexual game that they played out again and again. There seemed little love in this act more of a basic lust for battering and sexual rawness. Yet, this almost barbaric act seemed to thrill her, and she would walk around with such sexual confidence after, dropping out small details about her latest bottle battering. Laughing at how much she throbbed between her legs the next day and how the blackening bites up her legs and arms he'd given her were tokens of the thrill of the game. Her hard, crab surface would gleam with anticipation of his return night after night to begin the game again. He'd ring the doorbell and be shooed upstairs with such a speed that they rarely saw or heard him. They were then left following their progress through the thumps and whines coming from above.

'Jesus M, don't be so goddamn prudish' the Crab said after one of their nightly adventures when the Meerkat appeared at her door frowning.

'He's just a great goddam FUCK, who cares what anyone thinks' the Crab exploded.

'Come on C' the Meerkat said exasperated, unsure how she'd come to be the house spokesperson.

'The Elephant thought last night you were being strangled, she hardly slept'.

'Who gives a FUCK, none of her goddamn business' the Crab scowled. She then laughed to release the tension of the situation and showed the Meerkat a new bite. How the Tom could have mistaken this for love, the Elephant and the Meerkat never understood. Yet, the rejection and subsequent wine thrown over his head seemed to break his heart.

'There are so many things you just don't see' the Elephant said to the Meerkat shortly after the Tomcat episode.

What do you mean? The Meerkat asked, frowning.

'The bad things that are right in front of you' the Elephant said with a sigh. 'The Crab is filled with it.'

The difficulty was, the Meerkat was enthralled with the Crab's endless optimism and unusual, unpredictable behaviour. It had a strange addictive quality. It attracted enormous attention where ever they went and it felt good to be the centre of attention.

Balanced with the Crab's gregarious, hard side, she had a softer more maternal side. The Crab and the Meerkat between shifts at the restaurant would often sneak into her large double bed to watch old movies. They would dress in their fluffy, unflattering pyjamas, drink cheap white wine from thick-rimmed trucker mugs and gossip about their latest favourite male.

The Crab had previously rarely let anyone peer inside her hard inner shell and see this side of her nature. The shell she had adopted to help her survive. A shield around her body. Her childhood living alone with her abusive father had left her hard and unmoving, her mum had long been dead, having drunk herself to death. The Meerkat felt that she was the only one that got an occasional glimpse of the Crab's softer side. She wasn't the easiest friend to love, but there seemed to be deep compassion that she felt for the Meerkat, which over-rode her darker, obsessive side.

The Elephant looked on in dismay as the Crab and the Meerkat's friendship grew. Deep-down, her sense of the dark path it was taking filled the Elephant with fear. The only thing she saw every time she looked at the Crab wasn't the exotic, alluring individual but the red tough armour, formidable claws and her black beady eyes, intense and muddy against the backdrop of her vast, bright red hair. The Crab in-turn seemed to loathe the Elephant.

'I hate her far-fetched beliefs, most of it's bullshit' she told the Meerkat for the 100th time.

'She and her crazy theories make me sick to the stomach, what do you see in her?'

'Come on', the Meerkat replied. 'The Elephant is curious, intelligent and beautiful' she said.

Three of them living so closely in one place but only two friendships. Deep down the Meerkat knew that the Crab was jealous. She hated her for having other friends or lovers than her.

The Elephant keeps walking as the dogs keep barking.

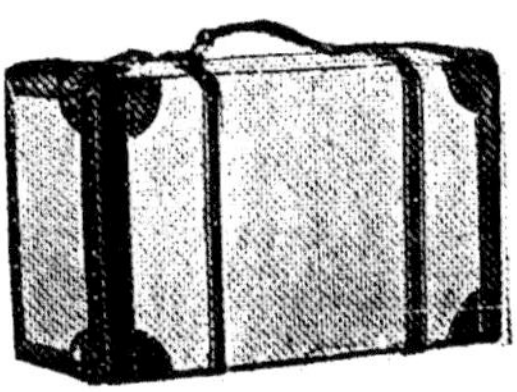

The Elephant was the first to leave the little house.

just leave her!' the Crab shouted at the Meerkat. She had quickly scrabbled out of the covers and stood high and alert on the headboard, listening intently at a vent in the wall.

They were watching a film, at a pause in a movie the Meerkat could hear the Elephant's low-frequency sobbing again. The Meerkat was sure they could both hear the Elephant, but the Crab, uninterested, proceeded to laugh at the movie.

'Ssh' the Meerkat said, trying hard to listen.

'She's such a melodramatic drama queen' the Crab snapped. She cast the Meerkat a disgusted sideways glance.

'What's wrong with her, have you got any idea?' the Meerkat asked.

The Crab frowned.

'Not a clue?'

Her eyes glazed over and she turned up the movie with the remote control, waving it around in the air in irritation.

'Jesus M, come down from there, you're making me giddy,' the Crab said.

The Meerkat scampered off the headboard, landed expertly on the floor and crawled back into bed guiltily.

The Elephant had become so quiet in the house that the Meerkat hardly noticed her anymore. Her beauty hidden behind long, limp unwashed hair. Her once proud cheeks, sunken and matt.

A week later, the Elephant packed her belongings and cleared out her room, sadness washed over her beautiful face when she approached the Meerkat to say goodbye.

'Why?' the Meerkat asked, with the same genuine surprise, for the 100th time. 'Why go?'

The Crab appeared from nowhere and whispered to the Elephant, 'You are such a drama queen' She laughed in the Elephant's face and the Meerkat could see the Elephant turn pale. 'what?' she asked, her eyes filled with disbelief. The Crab shuffled sideways and smiled. The Elephant's long eyelashes started to fill full of tears.

The Meerkat frowned at the Crab. 'I want to talk to her', she sighed. 'Alone' The Crab drummed her hand on the sideboard and then disappeared, laughing.

'Saw what?' the Meerkat asked.

'I'm sorry M, I'm going to miss you so much, but I need to go.' the Elephant sighed. 'Look, I can't talk about this right now' she said, as she finished packing her large grey trunk. 'I wish you'd come with me.' It was more of a question than a wish.

'I can't E, my life is heading in a different direction' the Meerkat said as she started to cry. The two of them gripped each other tightly sobbing, until the Elephant gradually pulled away and opened both her hands. The four wooden figures she'd found at the bottom of her trunk were tucked up inside.

'I'm sorry.' the Elephant said again, with tears in her eyes.

The Meerkat blinked at the four figures as the bile rose in her mouth.

Without the Elephant, the Crab and the Meerkat rented a tiny flat together in London. Without the Elephant, the Crab and the Meerkat's lives intertwined and wrapped around each other so tightly they were hardly ever apart. Without the Elephant, the Meerkat grew in a new way.

Years later, when the psychiatrist Doctor Drake sat the Meerkat down and told her the Crab was not her friend and never had been, the Meerkat wept like a bereaved lover.

The Chameleon

Chameleon

From Creaturepedia, the distinctively homemade (but well researched :) encyclopaedia

Chameleons don't change to fit in with their environment, they change colour to respond to light, temperature and their emotional state. Their range of colours can vary considerably from a variety of greens to reds, blue, pink, purple and all over grey. They are extremely timid and apart from their colour change are quite defenceless. Little is known about their life and habitats. They are very secretive, solitary creatures.

Description

They have remarkable eyes that rotate independently of each other, their brain can process two images simultaneously. They have a curious head bobbing action when breeding season is in full swing.

Warning:

Its emotional responses evoke the most unusual displays of colour, sometimes making them more conspicuous amongst their surroundings, not less. Chameleons tend to show brighter colours when displaying aggressively to other creatures and darker colours when they submit or 'give up'.

The Meerkat met the Chameleon in a gym steam room near Clapham Junction station. The day was cold, and there was a chill blowing in from the Baltic. The windows in the steam room were thick with condensation, and the heat rose and took the chill from her body.

"I'll be out in a minute', said the only thing in the room that had blended into the steam.

He had large, remarkable, beautiful green eyes with flecks of black, shiny skin and a much younger look than his years. He radiated a sharp intelligence but also an unconfident shyness. He made no effort to acknowledge the Meerkat as she entered the confined room. He just lay on his back, looking up at the ceiling basking in the heat and the steam. His face was flushing red, either from the heat or emotion she couldn't tell. She gave him her best smile and started a singing conversation. She'd always been told when she talked it sounded like she was singing. It was not a magical tune, instead a rise and fall of notes delivered at a fast tempo.

'Hello', she laughed.

'Something is tickling you?' he said and blushed an even brighter red. Incredibly slowly, he raised his head to look at her, his eyes flickered with amazement.

Her broad Yorkshire accent sounded odd contrasted against his rich, high-class southern tones. She had to pretend she was thinking of a joke. It wasn't an excellent one. Two robbers and a chicken.

'Oh, ha ha ha' he went. Laughter lines sprang over his face. The Meerkat thought it was nice to see his smile. 'That's good', he said. 'That's good'. With his intelligence and keen eyesight he missed not a thing.

She later found out that he'd been a border at a top London school. An outstanding student at Oxford. A straight-A star, 1st Class graduate with a very high IQ. A child prodigy. A model student. She'd never met anyone like him before, and she was intrigued.

The Fox & the Fawn

The Chameleon was born from an English mother and a Russian father, multimillionaires who gauged success by exam results, posh accents and a good, rich family name. Their fortune was gathered from old family money, it had been in their families for centuries. The Chameleon and all of his many siblings were both brilliantly bright and exceptionally beautiful. A successful result/ combination of well selected DNA. What was demanded from them all was success.

The Chameleon parents had met in a top nightclub in London when his father was studying applied maths at Cambridge University in the 1950s. His mother was as light, agile and beautiful as a delicate baby fawn. His father was an energic, dynamic, extroverted fox. The Fox was the offspring of a Russian wealthy tobacco producer who had excelled at maths from a very young age. He was then sent to England to learn British culture while getting a first-rate education in one of the world's top universities. He was awarded a first-class-honours in his final year and was mystified why the others in his year found the degree so hard. To him, maths came so naturally that he spent most of his time reading Victorian English literature rather than spending hours studying the most obvious maths books. The Fawn, the Chameleon's English mother, was a prominent, upper-society IT girl from London. A minor celebrity due to a modelling contract with a top London magazine. She had sex appeal and a uniquely engaging personality. Fame and beauty were perfectly balanced. Shoe shopping and party-going were her life. She was so stunningly beautiful and charming, that it was love at first sight for the Chameleon's father.

The Chameleon's father left Cambridge a year after the marriage when he got offered a top job as a stock-broker in the City. There, they quickly acquired money in such abundance that they couldn't spend it fast enough. Their huge mansion in the lush rolling Surrey countryside, with a pool and five horses, was the perfect space to entertain. As the Chameleon's mother's beauty faded over the years she spent all her money not on handbags and clothes but on facelifts and liposuction, until her face was so perfectly frozen in time it didn't move a millimetre. So much so it was hard to tell what she thought behind that perfect mask. Sometimes being born beautiful isn't a gift – especially when you have to watch it fade day by day.

The Chameleon's parents had only one thing in common, and that was the pressure they both applied on their two sons and two daughters to excel. All of the above was unbeknown to the Meerkat in their first few months together. She found it out slowly over a matter of time. But, like him, she felt their pressure for perfection from the first time she met them.

The Meerkat and the Chameleon emerged from Kensington tube station. From the hot hustle of the tube into a cold, rainy day. The Chameleon's mood had been dark that day, and the Meerkat was left unsure of what to say. They had hardly spoken since they'd left Golders Green. Sitting opposite her in the carriage, his face was grey, his lips were pinched, his hands were clasped and his eyes tightly shut as if trying desperately to remember a distant memory. In his silence, he blended into the seat. Suddenly he tapped on his watch with his short, sharp fingernail.

'We've got an hour to spare before the theatre' he said, 'what shall we do?' His voice was low and sulky. Only the week before he had arrived excitedly at her and the Crab's flat, waving two theatre tickets in her face and a bottle of beautifully wrapped, lavender perfume.

'This will be the best third date ever!' he'd said, seemingly eager to please when he'd shown her the tickets.

He was mysterious and unquantifiable. It didn't help that the Crab instantly and without reproach loathed him. She snapped at him every time he created a conversation. It was like a bad taste in her mouth when his name crossed her tongue.

The rain started to drip down onto her face, taking with it her meticulously applied eyeliner. She scampered under the green, projecting canopies of Harrods department store and waited for him to follow. The Chameleon just stood in the rain. His face was soaking in the large droplets. As he glanced to where she was standing, his large, green eyes, flickering, filled with water. The delicate shape of his face glistened, and for a fleeting minute, the Meerkat thought he looked quite beautiful, almost angelic.

'Let's head in there.' She gestured towards the entrance door of Harrods with her finger. He paused. Then with a rolling gait, swaying like he was imitating the motion of leaves in a breeze, he walked towards the door. Slowly he disappeared into the crowds.

'TOWARDS THE PIANOS!' he just managed to shout before he was gone from her sight.

With no idea where to go, she stooped down against the department store directory, staring in amazement at the labyrinth of spaces. Squinting, she had to lean further in. Out of breath, a whole twenty minutes later, she arrived, having got lost numerous times on the way. The Chameleon was standing against an ornate, plaster column, gazing over at the multitude of pianos. A vast forest of pianos, all shapes, colours and sizes. He was wearing a red silk scarf with tiny green flowers embroidered delicately into its fabric, wrapped around his neck. She'd never seen it before. His lips shimmered a light pink. Or was that just a reflection? She wasn't sure.

'Want to play?' the Meerkat said, winking as she approached, gesturing her arms over her curves and then elaborately flowing down onto one of the grand pianos. She was desperate to lighten the mood.

'Play...' His eyes lit up as he glanced hungrily over at the piano she was indicating, she was quickly forgotten. A black, impressive grand piano, like one of the ones she'd recently seen on the television in the Royal Albert Hall.

He stood smiling, caressing its white ivory keys with his delicate fingers. The Chameleon had brushed over in all their previous conversations his propensity or ability to play.

'I'm not great', he blinked quickly and laughed. The Meerkat was surprised by his quick change in mood.

The Chameleon sat down on one of the larger pianos, perching on the edge of the ornate wooden stool. She watched him stretch out his slender fingers and then he brushed over all of the keys in one sweep and flowed into a tune. She later learnt that he'd spent hours as a young boy practising. A labour of love, as opposed to the endless hours of law he studied to please both his parents.

As his fingers lightly bounced over the keys he seemed to change colour, the music flowed through his mind and body filling him with powerful emotions. The Meerkat hardly recognised him as he blended into the energy and opulence of the room. He was gracefully moving and swaying in time to the music, all carefully composed by his own delicate hands. As his music picked up pace, it radiated out across the room, calling to all the passing exotic crowds. When they first heard his music from afar, they were magnetically and hypnotically drawn to its sound.

They arrived like a flock of birds, flapping their wings, swaying, rolling and fluttering with each rising and falling note. The Chameleon, shining with glee at his ability to transfix and perform, bobbed his head with obvious delight. The real magic in play. When one song ended, the crowd stood still as everyone held their breaths for the next note. Intrigued by his musical nature and his sudden lack of shyness, the Meerkat stood quietly by, watching his transformation.

This was someone she could fall in love with, she thought.

Every spare minute the Meerkat wasn't with the Chameleon, she spent with the Crab. Neither was a tiny bit interested in the other. She couldn't believe that two people that were closest to her in her life hated each other so much.

One night, such a fun night, the Meerkat and the Crab accidentally left their shoes and coats in a nightclub. They had no idea where they had gone the next morning, or how they had come to leave them behind. The night was wild and out of control. It started with an enormous disagreement over a lost letter. It seemed to be the most critical thing in the Crab's life. The Meerkat had no idea who it was from.

'YOU'RE ALWAYS TIDYING!' the Crab shouted. 'I CAN'T LEAVE MY BLOODY MAIL ANYWHERE, IT'S SO FRUSTRATING.'

She was scurrying around the flat, throwing things in the air.

The Meerkat suspected that the bad mood was more over the fact that the Crab hated the Chameleon rather than over a lost letter. After the argument, the night had gained pace. A pace that had been an everyday occurrence earlier in their lives. A bottle of wine in the flat, comparing make-up, shoes and outfits. A walk to the nearest busy bar where they were welcomed in straight away by the eagle-eyed manager who plied them with fancy cocktails and chasers, his watchful, lustful eye on the Crab. Waiting for his chance.

'Sing, sing, sing!' they all chanted to the Crab.

She stood on the bar and sang in alluring tones. She was a real performer. Then onto a nightclub. The club had an enormous long queue of colourful individuals, all trying to stand out and be noticed. As the Meerkat, in her delicate, high shoes, raced to get to the back of the queue, she tripped. Then scrambled. Her fingers lightly brushed the floor, then, as she desperately tried to keep her balance, she slipped and crashed to the floor.

'Jesus!' the Meerkat shouted as she scrambled to her feet embarrassed. Her knees had started to pour with blood. When she looked up the Crab, in her amusement, was leaning against the wall laughing and watching the queue, for as the Meerkat had tripped, scrambled and crashed to the floor the crowd in unison with her every move had made the motion of a wave riding high in the air and then collapsing onto the shore.

They staggered home hours later, the Meerkat and the Crab, arm in arm, singing the same song. The letter, the argument, their coats and shoes had been forgotten. That's how it rolled.

2

It was late September. One of those beautiful, sunny days when the light is blue-gold and the trees are filled with red and green leaves. With their car windows down, the air, soft and warm stroked their faces. The Chameleon was quiet and withdrawn. The Meerkat lost in dangerous thoughts. The tension in the air was left unspoken and unresolved. The Meerkat loved the forest, this was where she felt most alive. The wood was an array of magical energy, a wealth of green and silver leaves dancing on the trees. As they entered the picnic area, someone started to sing. All attending the party were moved by the depth and soulfulness of the song, and everyone was still, filled with anticipation for the next verse.

At a pause in the song, the majestic form of the Bear quietly and softly moved into the clearing. He frowned in her direction as he sniffed her scent in the air. It had been years since she'd first seen him on the train. During this time, he'd grown into a man. He slowly sat down on a bale of hay next to a beautiful, cream-coloured, exotic cat. Her luscious fur flowed down her back, her high, movie star cheeks and full lips made her exquisite. She was padding his hand. Purring, softly contented. Laughing at his jokes. The Meerkat could tell she was in love. The surge of jealousy she felt overwhelmed her. She knew at that moment that she still had deep feelings for him, more than she wanted to admit.

As the Bear turned to face the Meerkat, she was instantly struck by such an intensity of desire. His familiar, chiselled face was still covered in hair but now peppered with tiny flecks of grey. She could feel a fundamental shift – she wanted to run her fingers through this hair. She knew she shouldn't, but she couldn't help but be more and more captivated by his gently pulsing energy. Everyone gathered around him as he told stories. He sang. He listened to troubled minds and brought a deep calmness to the setting. His energy, his humour, his laugh – he was magnetic. Did he remember her, she wondered?

When the food was laid out upon a large blanket on the forest floor, the only space left was next to the Bear. The Bear, with a big sandwich dripping with honey, was making a soft, content growling noise in the back of his throat. The Meerkat slumped down, resigned and troubled. His frosty stance was angled just in her direction. His back was turned. He was so close to her, with her keen sense of smell she could smell the honey and his familiar soft, warm, intoxicating scent and she struggled with an inherent longing to stroke his face and bury herself in his arms.

The Chameleon looked on and told her too loudly, 'Doesn't the Bear have tiny paws?' The Bear's enormous honey sandwich was stuffed into his mouth. With no subtleness the Chameleon pointed at the Bear's hands and laughed.

It grew dark, a fire pit was lit and the Bear gently ambled into the forest. The Meerkat's keen eyes watched him go. When the urge to follow became so overwhelming she couldn't resist, she crept through the trees, across a muddy path and onto an old ramshackle bridge. The considerable presence of the Bear filled the bridge. He paused and suddenly sniffed at the air as she walked closer.

'M, do you know how old the oldest tree is?' he softly growled, as she reached the bridge.

The wind blew a soft breeze onto her face, bringing with it his intoxicating scent.

'No' she said.

'9,500 years – a spruce in Sweden, 115 years times longer than a human being's lifetime. Creatures with such a luxury of time on their hands can afford to take things at a leisurely pace', he said. 'Quite remarkable', he sighed.

'I'm sorry, I had to leave and then I couldn't come back.'

'M, why are you here?' He asked. She didn't respond, how could she?

'I heard about your sister, I'm sorry, I could have helped, I wanted to help'. He placed his hands firmly onto the handrail of the bridge. The moss crept through his fingers and intertwined with the hair on his hands.

'No one could have helped' she murmured to herself. She said it so quietly she wasn't sure if he heard.

As she spoke, she could see his knuckles turn white as he gripped the handrail tightly, squeezing out all the moisture from the moss. The liquid dripped down into the stream below, making a small popping sound. She laid her left hand gently on top of his arm and stroked it. It felt good to touch him again. How she wished she could turn back time and sit on the train with him again, she was happier then. She wished she had met him before the Jackal – so many regrets and still so young.

He glanced down at her hand and the sparkling ring on her finger and looked up in disbelief. A tiny bit of her resented that he should find it a surprise. He didn't try that hard enough in those dark days. She bristled with anger.

'I'm glad you're happy now' he said and ambled away before she could say another word.

The dark, silhouetted high trees soon swallowed him up.

After the engagement and seeing the Bear again, her world changed. It didn't change for the Chameleon, their neighbours or the people she passed in the street. It wasn't that the Chameleon wasn't a worthy mate – he was. So what was wrong with her? Her life had shifted.

The Chameleon was still very quiet and withdrawn. It was like he had an aura around him, he'd become a shape she could see but couldn't quite touch. *Did he love her? Did he want this? Why was he so unhappy?* She tried to resume things the way they were before the engagement. She dressed in the morning. She took the tube into work. She bought milk on the way home. But no matter how many times she did these things, none of them seemed to have any weight or substance anymore. Questions kept going around and around in her head. The ring. The Bear. An enormous pressure on her mind. It felt fraudulent and futile.

They threw an engagement party, but Life didn't add up.

1 x large table + 15 individuals - 19 spoonsful of joy = - 4

The engagement party was held in an ancient, historical

hall in one of the best restaurants in the Meerkat's home town. It was wrapped in historical references: fake ancient tapestries, chunky wooden tables and chairs, Knights', shields and swords and coats of arms. A slowly decaying, dusty experience of a time so far away that it had no relevance anymore.

The Chameleon's parents and siblings had travelled up from Surrey. They sat to one side on their own, with their heads bobbing in whispering disagreement. The Meerkat's father stood silent. Still. Stiff. Uninvolved. Unmoved. Unemotional. He looked across the room and fixed his gaze on her and then at the ring on her finger. His eyes questioned her resolve to proceed with the charade.

To make matters worse, the Crab had refused to come. She was furious.

'What the fuck M?' the Crab shouted at her when she'd come around to the restaurant to confront her about the engagement rumour.

'Engaged!' she ranted. 'engaged!'

'Why not?' The Meerkat had challenged her. 'Why the HELL not?'

'Because you MAD cat...' she paused. ' Because you MAD cat'... she paused.

'Oh forget it, we both bloody know why.' she sighed. The Meerkat could see the anger in the Crab's eyes. Just a glimpse of hate flashed through them and then she blinked it away. The Meerkat didn't know why.

The Crab kept her distance for a whole lonely three months, no returned phone calls or texts – just silence.

'What do your parent think about all this?' The Meerkat asked the Chameleon suddenly one afternoon, when they were alone in the flat, both looking down at her ring.

His flat, stoned eyes suddenly flicked with a new intense energy, and he laughed.

'That is the multi-million-pound question, as my mother would say'. He giggled and went back to smoking the weed, forming round smoke circles high into the air.

'Have I mentioned the prenup yet?' he laughed. 'Mother's lawyer sent it through in the post, it's on the side, take a look.' He waved his hand casually in the direction of the table and closed his eyes.

After that, she knew for sure. Her world fell apart. Within weeks, she'd shrunk two dress sizes, and her hair started to fall out as she chewed it away. She bit her nails for the first time in years and developed cold sores that extended from her lip to the inside of her nose. In her rage one night over their predicament, she walked into the lounge door frame and knocked herself out. She'd come home, and the Chameleon was stoned again. Lost in his own world, one that she was not allowed to enter. When she came to, a concerned Chameleon peered into her face with his large dead lenses and ghost smile. Her eye had started to swell and throb.

'Are you ok M?' he asked, stroking her face with his hand. She placed her hand on top of his and pressed it close to her face. She hadn't felt that hand on her face for a very long time.

3

The Chameleon and the Meerkat had been invited to a New Year's Eve house party. It was a hat party. She was not wearing a hat. No hat, one black eye, a cold sore, where had she gone?

They had walked across the road to her friend's house in silence. She was miserable, and she sensed he was too. She didn't know who he was any more. They arrived at the large Victorian flat in silence. She could see through the window that the party was in full swing. The music was booming. The drinks were flowing. The room was filled with strange hats, flirting, dancing, laughing and moving along with the music. The atmosphere was electric, and everyone they could see was happy and staggeringly drunk. They stood together at the large Victorian door and paused. Should they go in? They looked at each-other's miserable faces in unison and nodded, and the Meerkat knocked on the door. The door was instantly opened by a large Smurf with a painted blue face. The laughter, music and smell of the alcohol overwhelmed their senses as they walked into the expansive hall. The party was in full swing. The lounge, the kitchen and the hallway were filled with individuals dancing, wearing crazy hats and bright clothes. Everyone was wild, dancing with their fists pumping in the air.

As the crowd parted to let them through, the first person she recognised was the Bear. Her heart skipped a beat. The intensity of her entrapment felt even more acute. A deep, sensual pulling sensation rose in her stomach as she watched him. The Bear was dressed in a black suit, a crisp white shirt and a black tie, with an orange children's balaclava style bear hat. Its tiny orange ears stood proud on his head, jiggling as he laughed. He was holding court, surrounded by creatures, long-legged females and dapper, designer males with shaven heads and long beards. She suddenly wished she'd brought a hat. She stood there instead, invisible, sullen and trapped. She'd heard that the Bear had broken up with the beautiful blonde from the picnic. A small gingery curvy creature had taken her place by his side, hanging from his arm and rubbing his leg. She found herself at his side. She knew her time was short, the Chameleon's eyes missed nothing. She walked straight up to the Bear. Unplanned she blurted out,

'Can we talk? I need to explain.' she implored him with her eyes. 'Come around to our flat for dinner?'

It sounded insane even as she said it, he looked vaguely surprised and then turned away.

Timeline: Spring

'Come over to EVE and meet the new boss tomorrow at 2pm, he will decide, sorry what's your name again?' the voice down the phone asked her.

'M' She said, for the third time. She heard him scribble her name down this time – a scratching sound against a hard surface.

'We have a vacancy for a chef M, but it's the boss who decides. He decides everything' the voice grumbled. 'Oh, and don't be late: he hates lateness.' He ended the call without a goodbye.

The Meerkat's latest job wasn't working out. She'd overheard her boss saying, 'M's an outstanding chef but high maintenance.' Her amazing cooking didn't compensate for a fading black eye and a miserable face. The Chameleon had lost his job as a lawyer a few weeks before. His weeks off work had finally ended in his dismissal. He'd looked happy when he'd told her. So, rather than wait to be fired, she'd started looking around for a new job. Bills littered the floor of their flat waiting to be paid – neither one of them picking them up.

Eve was a new trendy night club and restaurant that everyone was raving about. She needed to drop in at 2pm after the lunchtime rush at work was over.

But she was late, very late. 2:15pm. A very last-minute order that the waitresses shouldn't have taken forced her into a panic. When she'd finally finished, she rushed around getting ready, taking off her apron, brushing down her jeans, stroking back her hair and throwing on her old parka coat with a large brown bushy, furry hood. 2:25pm. She ran up the road and rushed in through a huge, wooden antique doors and down the stairs into the club. 2:30pm.

A tall man appeared in her vision as she ran panting down the final few stairs. He stood with his back towards her, bending over an old-fashioned pinball machine – smashing the balls around the table.

'YOU'RE LATE' he growled over his shoulder.

In her panic, she missed the last step. She tumbled. She flew. She hit the floor at speed. Flat on her front, she slid rapidly across the expansive, shiny dance floor. Her furry hood flopped over her head, burying her in its fur. When, finally, the momentum of her fall slowed she lay still, her red face pressing against the damp floor. She waited to be swallowed up.

Hands suddenly grabbed her under her arms, a laugh and then a deeper harder laugh as she was pulled to her feet. She stood, face fully covered, hot with shame. He laughed hard again, a deep, throaty roar.

She peeled back her hood and tentatively peered out.

'You're hired!' he laughed and gave her a round of applause. 'Amazing entrance, well done.' He stopped clapping and held out his long, slender hand. 'Welcome to EVE'.

Her heart stopped.

'I'm the owner', he confirmed into her shocked and confused eyes.

She looked at his chiselled, handsome face in shock – the Jackal.

Calm and so incredibly confident. There was still an air of unexpected slyness around him. The Meerkat, in her jeans and t-shirt, paled against his crisp, pinstriped suit with a stark, white-collared shirt.

'My, my, it has taken years for us to meet again', he said. 'How surprised I was when my general manager told me you'd called', he said. 'Why did you leave so quickly and never come back? You never even returned my calls, tut, tut.' He stroked his tie with his hand as he spoke.

'I couldn't return.' she said.

'Why, pray tell me?' the smile turned into a cold sneer.

'Too hurtful.' The Meerkat waved her hand to silence him and blinked away the tears that had sprung up from her eyes.

'Yes, sorry about that', he said. 'I did hear what happened.' Anguish appeared across his face, and his frosty gaze softened. She wiped her eyes with the back of her hand. He glanced at the ring on her hand, blinked in surprise and abruptly changed the conversation.

'TWO COFFEES, NOW!' he shouted angrily over to a nearby waitress, who quickly scampered off behind the bar.

The Jackal (he told her) was now the model father of a beautiful young son and the husband of an exotic raven with a property tycoon father. The Meerkat suspected that, rather than hard work, was the source of the money for the club they now sat in. He had a new, confident air in his manner, and the boy she once knew was gone.

'My wife's beauty is legendary' he repeatedly told her. 'I'm so proud that I managed to snare her' he laughed.

As the interview progressed, the Meerkat felt like she was meeting an old, valued friend again, not a disruptive lover.

'I'm always here for you M' he repeated, with a caring, fatherly smile, 'you only need to ask and I'll help in any way I can', with a pat, pat, pat on her hand. 'Let's make this fun, life is too short!' he laughed.

'I don't know what to say', she said. As they continued to talk, he made her feel so incredibly at ease that she accepted the job with excitement.

Over the next few months, they grew to be friends. Jackals are highly strung creatures that tend to get wilder as they mature. His temper was short and hardly controlled. He would spend hours sitting in the kitchen, laughing at her turmoil and complimenting her baking. He would take off his jacket, roll up his sleeves and get her to teach him how to make the perfect cake or truffle, never tiring or not having enough time. But then he'd shout at the bar and waitress staff till they shook in fear for the tiniest mistake.

'Why a nightclub?' she asked him one afternoon.

'It suits me, being a nocturnal creature', he laughed. 'Remember when we first met, M?' He casually asked her.

'How could I ever forget?' she smiled. She was surprised, even to this day, that she had caught his eye. 'For me, not drinking alcohol was always a problem with my friends. My parents in the Salvation Army would just never allow it. How things have changed!' she laughed.

It was a typical Saturday night, and she was still only fifteen. Unbeknown to her parents, she ended up meeting her friends in a bar. It was one of the less classy bars in town. As she waited on the sidelines, she watched her friends get drunk. As she watched and waited, she was constantly deflecting conversation from drunk males looking left and right for someone to take home that evening. Then a different kind of male approached her – he was very handsome. He wasn't slurring his words, so she thought he would be a perfect buffer. Time went by, and he asked for her number. He was so charming, she gave him her real one and didn't overthink it, for he was out of her league. The very next day, he called her, much to her and her friend's surprise.

'You were the only sober male in our town', she laughed.

'You were the only sober female' he frowned. 'It doesn't do to lose control M, does it?' he added seriously, 'I had big plans and needed to be out of that small-minded town, and now look at me.' he waved his arm around the club, all fluffed up and territorial.

EVE was growing into a huge success. The Jackal bought two new EVE franchise models in Dubai and New York, never tiring of working, filled with ambition. Soon the Meerkat and the Jackal were travelling the world together, working with big corporate clients, running prestigious events, never tiring and always on call 24/7. It was like nothing had ever happened between them in the past and she felt safe. Work became her life.

Much to the Chameleon's despair.

The Crab, well she adored him. She swept into EVE one evening on the way to a ball. She had on a beautiful, red, see-through lace evening dress and her hair was pinned high on her head in soft, sensuous curls. The Meerkat heard the commotion from the kitchen.

'WHERE IS SHE? WHY IS SHE HERE ALL THE TIME?' The Crab asked in a loud, demanding voice.

'Who?' Said the Jackal, laughing. The Meerkat could see the Jackal soak up the Crab's curves and passionate nature in a devouring glance.

'We, both know who, are you keeping her chained to the radiator?' The Crab laughed, 'Or is she here by choice? Because I've not seen her for months.' As she asked, she stood back and weighed up the Jackal. 'My, my, I believe we have met before' she smiled.

The Jackal frowned, held out his hand and suddenly pulled the Crab close and whispered in her ear. The Meerkat at that moment felt a twinge. Was it jealousy? No, she was sure she was beyond all of that. Did the Crab know him? She was confused.

'No, no, don't get me wrong, you did me a favour', the Crab said as she laughed and pulled away, making a gesture to signal she wanted a drink.

'Gin and tonic with grapefruit', she added, 'and plenty of ice'. Then she stretched out on one of the plush banquette seats, her long, slender legs glimmering in the light of the club. She patted the seat next to her, mischievously. The Jackal took the bait and folded beside her.

The Crab never went to the ball. The Meerkat stayed in the kitchen. She could hear them laughing over the sound of the music. At one point, the Crab stood up and sang to the crowd. Her soft, alluring singing voice filled the kitchen with its magic and even the waitresses stopped to stare – the Jackal clearly captivated. When the Meerkat occasionally glanced over from the safety of the kitchen, the Jackal would wink and smile, and she would be cross with herself. Cross with her own inbuilt curiosity.

'Quite an amazing, colourful character', the Crab told her later, when she'd finished her shift. 'A bit more control now he's grown more mature', she laughed, 'but clearly infatuated with you, my dear'.

The Meerkat stood by the banquette seat with her hair dishevelled, her jeans ripped and her eyes dark and tired. The Crab still looked fresh and glamorous.

'Have you met him before?' the Meerkat asked, confused.

'Before, before?' the Crab rolled the word around her tongue like a song.

'Why ever did you let him go, what a catch!' the Crab laughed with a glint in her eye.

'Before?' the Meerkat asked again.

The Crab, bemused, swiftly whipped up her bag and marched out.

After that, the Meerkat heard the Jackal and the Crab had become friends. Or maybe more.

Timeline: Winter

'When's the big day?' The Jackal casually asked her one day when eyeing her ring.

She paused. His question took her by surprise. They had never spoken about her ring or the Chameleon before.

'I'm not so sure when' she said.

'Not so sure when, or not so sure?' He asked, slyly.

Perched on a stool in the kitchen, his black, tailored, crisp suit and white shirt made a sharp contrast to the stainless-steel surfaces and white walls. His casual voice and laid-back manner took her off her guard.

'Both'. She sighed.

He jumped off the stool in surprise and came and stood very close to her. 'Look, this isn't right to talk about here.'

She sighed and started to cry.

'M, I'm always here for you.' He wrapped his arm around her shoulder and pulled her close. She could smell the familiar scent of his body.

'He hardly looks at me or talks to me anymore, I don't know what to do', she said. 'He's so distant and uninterested, quiet and consumed.' She looked down at her ring as a tear dripped from her nose.

'Wow, I remember', the Jackal said when he'd recovered from his shock, 'how excited I felt when I asked my wife to marry me, I wanted to spend the rest of my life with her – she simply enchanted me.' He smiled, while the Meerkat's misery grew by the minute.

'I felt so in love', he said. 'It was the best feeling in the world.' He paused and stroked the Meerkat's hand. His face was etched with concern. He tightened his grip on her shoulder. Instead of the friendly, comforting words, she was expecting, he whispered:

'I suppose, I don't have to tell you how lovely you are.' He caressed her spine and she felt nothing inside or out, just his hand on her back. It occurred to her then, that she had not been touched for a very long time. With tearful eyes, and her make-up all smudged, she started to apologise to the Jackal.

'I'm sorry, what did you say?' she said. He then wrapped his other arm around her and held her face in his hands.

'I suppose, I don't have to tell you how lovely you are.' he repeated.

He then leaned in for an unexpected kiss. He pushed himself against her body.

'What!' she pushed him away in surprise.

'My wife is always wearing yoga gear and drinking white wine' the Jackal sighed, as if to explain his behaviour somehow. 'I love you M, in fact, I've never stopped loving you' he said in a calm, level voice.

She stepped back in bewilderment. The façade dropped from his face, and she was looking and hearing someone she knew from her past. When, later, she returned to her flat and crawled into bed next to the still almost frozen Chameleon, he texted her dozens of times, telling her how happy he was that his feelings for her were finally out in the open. The Chameleon shifted around in the bed in unison to the bleeps of the in-coming texts.

I love you M. Come back to EVE and see me.

Please.

I've always wanted you.

You must have known.

I thought you felt it too...

She ignored them all.

Otter

From Creaturepedia, the distinctively homemade (but well researched :) encyclopaedia

An otter is a shy creature by nature, but they're extremely territorial.

Description

Otters have long, slim bodies and small limbs. Otters are playful and appear to engage in various behaviours for sheer enjoyment, such as making waterslides. Different species vary in their social structure, with some being largely solitary, while others live in groups.

Warning:

Otters might look soft and cuddly, but remain dangerous animals. Sometimes they are way too playful and tickle you till you cry. Watch these sneaky fellows.

tter

4

Timeline: Winter

'No L, I can't possibly go, NO-way,' the Meerkat sighed. 'I have the biggest cold sore possible.' She breathed heavily into her phone.

The coldsore stretched across her top lip and up into her nose. It looked like a fake, comedy Hitler moustache, and everyone felt the inherent need to point it out to her, even though it was humming with pain on her face, constantly reminding her it was there. She still hadn't confronted the Chameleon, and she was feeling dreadful most of the time. She had lost sixteen pounds, and her body was telling her it was not happy by rewarding her with this vast, uncontrollably growing cold sore that had gathered a throbbing, pulsating life of its own. Then, unexpectedly, a text from the BEAR:

The otter

TEXT: Fancy coming to my birthday?

7:30/8, Saturday night at the Red Bar on Poland Street, Soho. The Bear

She couldn't go, could she? The coldsore throbbed its confirmation, NO. But, just maybe, she had to? The Otter was coming to stay, and was keen for a London night out.

'Come on M, it will be fun, we have to go' the Otter said again into her mobile.

'Is the handsome Bear still single?' he giggled. She laughed, 'You're not quite his type!'

She was so desperate to feel a glimpse of happiness again. Torn, she wobbled and decided to go. The Red Bar in Soho was one of those crazy, exciting places in London. The bar was unbelievably busy, there was hardly room to stand up. People were knocking and swaying into each other. Ten minutes after their arrival, the Bear briefly came over.

'Great moustache, M' he said, laughing, waving his single finger under his nose.

He then bounded back into the crowd. At this point, and at other equally stressful points of her life, the MeerKat's drinking got out of control. She simply didn't care. She aimed to get as drunk as possible, as quickly as possible and this was one of those nights. She drank. It was hot. She drank. It was crowded. She drank. She was sweeping up discarded drinks from tables in her desperate state. She lost her ability to talk and listen as she drank more and more.

The Otter was busy. The last time she saw him, how long ago she was not sure, he was chatting to a bright, young thing dressed in white, fawning over him like an expectant lover. The Meerkat's head started to throb. The alcohol was draining out all of her body's moisture. Feeling suddenly sick, she raced off to the toilet to get some tap water. Trip, trip, tripping down the stairs, tumbling down twenty, thirty stairs to the basement on her bottom, cracking the heel of her shoe in the process. At the bottom of the stairs, she sat on the cold, wet floor and cried and laughed to herself in a sad, drunken haze.

When eventually she managed to stand and go into the

bathroom, she looked into the mirror. The person looking back at her was crazy. The black of the coldsore, the black of her make-up spilling down her face.

'Well done M, well done', she slurred to her refection and slipped back down onto the floor. Everything was looking and feeling black.

After an hour of lying on the toilet floor, she eventually managed to crawl back up the stairs, with black make-up smeared all around her tearful face. From the corner of her eye, she noticed the Bear. He was kissing a dark-haired individual at the bar with enormous breasts.

The Jackal, watching her anguish from the bar, sensing her loneliness and vulnerability, crept in and again took her sensibility.

Timeline: Winter

'Tomorrow morning, let's stop and set a date for our wedding' the Chameleon said quietly one winter's day, when she crawled in from work. His lips moved, but his body stayed remarkably still.

The next morning before he woke, she rushed into work. During the night, she'd had three panic attacks. The desire to be honest with the Chameleon hummed in her brain. The anxiety was paralysing. In her numbness and fragility, she panicked and did something stupid, always to regret. A simple text to the Elephant.

Text: E, he doesn't love me. I don't know what to do? X

Text: E, I can't keep this going anymore, I think his parents think I want his money x

There was no response from E, no comfort, she waited. Impulsively she texted again.

Text: E, I don't know if this is love anymore – how can I marry him with things like this? X

TEXT: **THIS IS ME.** Texted back the Chameleon.

TEXT: **THIS IS ME, M.**

Panic. Gasp. Shock at her carelessness and the madness of it all. She returned back to their flat later that night, and he was lying in his red hammock, swinging in the dark night.

'I'm so sorry.' is all she could say, as she watched their lives fall apart.

'I'm sorry too.' he whispered back into the night.

They had a flat, a cat and a load of old furniture. All needed portioning out and splitting. She also had to manage the fall-out from a bunch of bewildered friends. All who couldn't believe what they had done. The 'Mad Meerkat' became her nickname, whispered behind her back even by her closest friends.

'How can they split up? The perfect couple, I bet that Jackal is to blame' she heard them whisper.

'If everyone lines up around the world in a big long queue' her dad had said when she rang him despairing, 'you'd be the last person in the line able to help him through this.' He was stern in his effort to get her to pull herself together. 'You need time apart, I'm sorry M, I really am.'

'We can't keep living together in this flat' she quietly told the Chameleon one evening, as he lay outside in the hammock. She wanted to find comfort and peace. He blended into the fabric of the hammock. Swinging back and forth. Back and forth.

'WE CAN'T KEEP LIVING TOGETHER IN THIS FLAT' she shouted into the air. He didn't respond, just swung back and forth like he didn't have a care in the world.

'TALK TO ME!' she yelled into the darkness and stormed off to work, only to be watched by the Jackal, who was monitoring her every move.

The Meerkat heard much later that the Chameleon was raced into hospital to have his stomach pumped. The fifty tablets he'd taken were slowly shutting down his organs, and it was hit and miss if he would survive.

She didn't know this at the time. In fairness to him, he didn't tell her, he just returned to their flat having been missing for a while, looking thinner and more miserable than ever. Her relief that he'd not been around for days was replaced with dread and concern when she saw his face that day. She was now responsible for a person not wanting to live. She wanted to comfort him, but a wall had gone up.

They lived together for way too long while they sorted out the splitting of their joint things. Both living in hope. Both residing in anxiousness. She stayed in the flat. He moved back in with his parents, who couldn't help enough to assist with his moving out. But he wanted everything inside the flat, he told her.

Even her poor, limited, Wham CD selection.

'You've got yourself in trouble again', said the Elephant. She sat at the end of the Meerkat's bed, exhausted from an overnight flight from India. Half an hour before, they had rushed into each other's arms.

'I miss you so much', the Meerkat sobbed. 'Am I going mad?' she sighed. She placed her head in Elephant's hands.

The next morning, the Elephant thundered into her room. 'Come on M, I want to show you something extraordinary!' she said. They travelled on the underground down to the South Bank. They walked on the bank of the river and looked into its blue, silvery glow. The sun was just dipping behind the earth, casting a soft, orange halo. The Elephant had learnt from her Buddhist teachings something special. As they walked, she described to the Meerkat that the relationships you build around you form invisible bonds that bind you to the people you care for and love.

'Look' the Elephant said. The Meerkat glanced at the crowds walking up and down the paths next to the river.

'Imagine we are all connected' the Elephant said in wonder. 'Imagine, if you could see those connections like red ribbons attached to each other, how amazing would that be!' her face glowed. The Elephant paused and looked into the Meerkat's confused face.

'But, where there is light there is always darkness', she continued, 'sometimes these connections go black and toxic, ribbons once red become broken and black – do you get what I mean?' she said.

The Meerkat shook her head.

'You can't help it M, it's out of your control, your can't make him love you, don't you see that?' The Elephant paused; maybe she thought she'd been too hard.

The Meerkat sat down on the bench and cried. The Elephant pulled her into her arms and back from the brink, stroking her hair with soft, comforting hands. The Meerkat felt truly loved, and that love shook the black ribbons from around her neck just enough so she could breathe again.

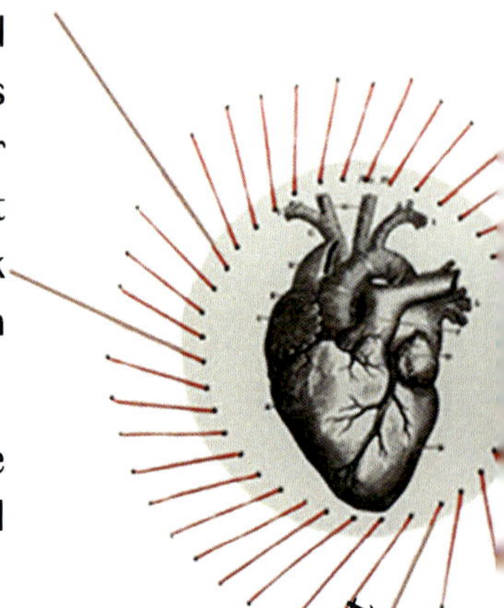

'You have to follow your heart, M'. the Elephant told her later when she'd stopped crying.

'I know', the Meerkat sobbed, 'but it's so hard, I do love him.'

'People can love in different ways,' the Elephant said gently.

'You can love full-on, with lots of noise, or you can do it quietly, over a cup of tea. You can even love, without them knowing it'.

'You can love full-on, with lots of noise, or you can do it quietly, over a cup of tea.

A tiny bit of guilt stirred in the Meerkat's stomach as the Bear's image appeared in her mind.

The Elephant had found a spiritual path that for her led to a world of possibilities. No one noticed the road she was on until she had walked well down it, everyone else was too busy with their western lives and values to notice. She was learning to become enlightened and, in this journey, she found a calmness that no one had ever seen before.

The Meerkat envied her.

The path the Elephant took allowed her to grow and learn and she became calmer and content, reliable and dependable but she still maintained a wild, travelling spirit that meant no one quite knew where she was in the world at any one point in time. While all their friends were building pension plans, buying homes, thinking of having children and racing hard up some perceived important career path, the Elephant lived in some dusty hostel or campsite, carrying all of her life's possessions around in her enormous old grey trunk. In the French mountains, in the streets of Mumbai or in a cave retreat in the Himalayas she would wander, looking to find her true self. People around her, her family and friends, didn't understand this path she had decided to take.

the Elephant would wander looking to find her true self.

Regularly enough to keep their friendship burning brightly she would appear on the Meerkat's doorstep for a night, where they would immediately start the conversation off at precisely the same point as they'd left it weeks or months before. There was never any frustration that neither of them had emailed or called enough during that period of absence, there were no promises or commitments made. They both knew that they had a bond and therefore, would see each other soon. Soon was just never defined.

Those, to the Meerkat, were the best type of friendships: no guilt, no high expectations or jealousy, just genuine love.

The Jackal, never one not to get his own way, had developed an intensity of feeling for the Meerkat that was suffocating. He circled her like prey.

The split from the Chameleon had strengthened his resolve to control. He was charming, charismatic and intense. He'd spend hours standing in EVE's kitchen watching her bake. When he wasn't standing by her, he would repeatedly text her in the early hours of the morning, mainly when drunk. Always swinging wildly between seductive tones and frustrated shouting.

Text: 'I love you M, come on, call me back' he'd say.

Text: call me back ASAP jx

Text: where the FUCK are you :-(

Then one day, the Jackal brought in a woman to dine.

To humiliate her, or to make her jealous? The Meerkat weighed it up from the safety of the kitchen.

'Darling, you must meet one of my head chefs', she heard the Jackal say too loudly.

'Oh my God *no*, how could he?' the Meerkat fumed. The game had begun.

'M, M come over to the table', the Jackal waved at her. He'd clearly spotted her trying to scurry away into the storage room.

'Oh, and bring us some of those amazing truffles you make', he instructed.

She cringed. Approaching the table a few minutes later she first noticed her lustrous, long, wavy black hair glistening with a dark blue velvet sheen. The Jackal had his arm draped around her neck and was stroking her naked arm. He then whispered something into her ear.

'Come, come we've not got all day!' the Jackal barked at the Meerkat.

'Hi', he then casually said as she approached, 'meet my wife – the Raven'.

Raven

From Creaturepedia, the distinctively homemade (but well researched :) encyclopaedia

Ravens are one of the most intelligent birds in the world. They have a mischievous nature and can be known to mock or taunt. In Greek mythology, ravens are associated with Apollo, the god of prophecy. They are said to be a symbol of bad luck, and were the gods' messengers in the mortal world.

Description

The raven spirit animal symbolizes your intelligence and your ability to learn quickly. You use what you learn to figure out solutions to your problems. The raven totem signifies mystery and divination, and the attraction to the magical or mystical ways

Warning:

Collective nouns for a group of ravens (or at least the common raven) include 'unkindness', 'treachery' and 'conspiracy'.

R
a

'Oh, you have got a mischievous nature,' the Jackal laughed as he nibbled the Raven's neck.

The Raven giggled. In his crisp, black suit, slicked-back gelled hair and chiselled face, he looked startlingly handsome. The Raven on his arm was a magnificent thing. The Meerkat's eyes soaked in her beauty – it was hypnotic.

The Raven had a sharp, but beautiful, distinguished nose with a delicate diamond piercing

Bright red luscious lips.

Elegant and pointed black glossy nails.

Toned, thin, olive legs.

A long, tight-fitted black dress that cupped her ample breasts.

A long, black cloak with a fan-shaped tail.

Intelligent black eyes with thick, luscious eyelashes.

She was sensual, sexual and captivating. Diamonds hung from her, twinkling and sparkling: rings on her hands, bracelets running up her arms, necklaces hanging from her neck and one single diamond in her nose. The Meerkat brushed the flour from her apron and stood up straight and alert with a silver truffle plate in her hand.

'Darling, the Jackal here tells me what an amazing, adventurous baker you are.' She paused as she weighed up the Meerkat standing in front of her. 'Mmmm, in fact, I need to keep my eye on him, because he talks about you a little too much.' She tightly smiled and pouted in the Jackal's direction.

The Jackal howled with laughter and kissed the Raven on her tightly-closed lips. The Raven paused. Then she lifted one of the delicate truffles in her long elegant fingers, sniffed it with her fine structured nose and then hungrily sucked at its side until it slowly slid into her mouth and disappeared between her red lips. The Jackal watched her in admiration.

'Delicious.' The Raven said. She paused and flapped her hands in the air.

'But, my darling much more butter is needed, tut, tut' she mocked.

The Meerkat stood, shocked. The Raven turned back to the Jackal and started humming a little sensual tune, maybe a song they shared because it made the Jackal smile. What seemed like hours later, but was only a few minutes, the Raven turned back to the Meerkat almost surprised that she was still standing there.

'Thanks, you can go', the Raven gestured with a flick of her hand – which was her true nature talking.

As the Meerkat turned away, she heard the Raven saying, making sure she could hear:

'Why darling, you never mentioned she was quite so delicious and edible.' She looked at him with a questioning eye.

'Not quite to my taste', the Jackal replied.

Change the channel if you don't like the programme.

The Meerkat understood the desperate need to change the channel. Do something.

It didn't need to be ambitious. She looked out of her window.

She made up her bed with crisp, white sheets.

She folded one pair of dish towels.

She separated the big forks from the little ones.

Every life is hard, sometimes, she kept thinking. Do what you need to do.

Change the channel.

She straightened one shelf of books.

She placed all her books into colour blocking – reds with reds, blue with blues.

She washed out the glass sugar bowl with crumbs in the bottom.

Maybe she should do her own thing?

Change the channel.

She stroked her cat one hundred times and counted.

She dusted the top of her picture frames.

She rolled her knickers into tiny balls in her drawers.

Maybe she should be her own boss?

Changing the channel is OK.

She had the controller in her hand, but a flurry of worries rocked her mind, making her go around and around in tiny circles... fear is death, death is fear, fear is death.

Will I be able to pay my mortgage?

Am I good enough?

Will I go bankrupt?

Am I good enough?

... round, and round, and round.

Change the channel.

Then one day, she realised. If she didn't change the channel, she was going to go mad. So as scary as it was, she pressed the button and allowed herself to imagine a new world with herself in it. Maybe then, just maybe, she would smile again.

A new idea then gradually formed in her creative mind.

Instead of phone calls and texts, the Meerkat was following the Crab's life via social media. The last time she had seen the Crab was in EVE. That had hurt. She had witnessed the Crab and Jackal together, and it had taken her by surprise. The energy and chemistry between them was hard to ignore. *How did they know each other?* she asked herself over and over again. But, why should she care, she repeatedly thought to herself.

The Crab was busy in her new life, yachting around the Maldives. The Crab's love for hot places and soft sandy beaches fulfilled to the fullest. The Meerkat had seen on Facebook a raft of photos of her new life: the Crab looking sexy on a boat with a young crowd, the Crab sunbathing in a yellow and white spotted bikini on a soft, sandy beach, the Crab at a beach party holding an elaborate cocktail. In one of the Crab's latest posts, the Meerkat was sure she could see the Jackal leaning against a railing at the back of the boat, surrounded by lots of beautiful creatures.

His absence from EVE wasn't missed.

The Crab's life was so far removed from the hot kitchens the Meerkat lived in. So fascinating and enchanting. With a new curiosity in her mind after she saw the latest picture, she texted the Crab.

Text: C, I've not seen you for ages, fancy meeting for lunch? Mx

Text: M, I'm back in London next week, I'd love to meet up, let's meet at The Ivy, my treat for your last birthday – sorry I didn't send a card, you know how busy I am LOL Cx

Text: I'd love to. Mx

As glamorous as the Crab's life seemed on Facebook, she was actually bored and soaked up the story about the Chameleon with delight.

'Poor baby' the Crab stated. The Meerkat was unsure if she was referencing her or the Chameleon. 'He always was so, so incredibly predictable and perfect don't you think?' the Crab said.

'He's a good man, and I do love him', the Meerkat replied defensively.

'Slightly asexual, don't you agree?' The Crab said laughing.

The Meerkat frowned, this was not a conversation to be had with the Crab. No sympathy there. The Meerkat glanced around the crowded restaurant and waited for the Crab to stop laughing. She crossed her arms and waited.

'And how's the lovely Jackal?' the Crab asked.

'I don't know', the Meerkat said, cutting the conversation short. 'Do you?'

The Crab blushed. 'Hardly my dear', she laughed again and waved her hand at the waitress 'Another gin and tonic, with grapefruit and ice' she said, way too loud. 'M, another?' she asked, pointing at the Meerkat's empty glass. She always tried to get the Meerkat drunk when she wanted to get information out of her, it was a pattern that frustrated the Meerkat, she didn't need any encouragement.

'No, I'm fine with water thanks', the Meerkat said abruptly.

The waitress came over with a large, bronze tray with two small, delicate glasses perched in the middle. She passed the gin and tonic to the Crab.

'Not enough ice' the Crab snapped 'Damn it'. The waitress turned and dashed back to the bar. 'Service is poor here these days – now where were we?'

The Meerkat took a sip of her water. 'Look, I'd like to tell you about my new venture', the Meerkat said. 'A new type of baking thing'. She paused, waiting for the Crab's reaction. 'I've even got an idea for a name', said the Meerkat. 'Devour, what do you think?'

The Crab licked her lips and clapped with glee. '"Devour" how lovely', she laughed. 'I love it.' She said 'M, we'd be unstoppable together, why not?' The Crab looked at her in eagerness, the boredom had fallen from her eyes. 'But you don't know what it is yet.' the Meerkat sat back in surprise, as the Crab highlighted her real life behind the glossy Facebook photos.

'I'm bored M, I need more fun and adventure, his lordship has a tight control of my spending these days – he is far less generous now than when we first got together, I can't even buy a new car, and I've had mine for over a year!' The Crab said in disgust.

The Meerkat laughed.

'With our endless joint energy and your skills, we will be unstoppable' The Crab clapped her hands with glee. So, one rainy morning the following week, 'Devour' was registered as a limited business with two shareholders. The Crab contributed all of the money and connections and the Meerkat her skill and experience.

'I'm leaving', the Meerkat said to the Jackal that very afternoon.

She placed her resignation letter into his hand. They were all alone in his office, his face looked murderous.

'Where are you going?' He asked. He placed his pen down and stared directly at her.

'Look, it's really none of your business', she said. 'We're done.'

'M, you know I care about you' he said, 'I've always wanted the best for you', he sighed. 'Sit down let's talk about this?' He patted his lap.

'Look, there is no point' she sighed. 'I've made up my mind, the Crab and I are going into business – a partnership.' He looked at her with frosty eyes. 'The Crab', he mumbled to himself.

'Pathetic, it won't work' he scowled. 'Well, let's see', the Meerkat said, and turned to leave.

'YOU CAN'T GO!' he shouted, as she walked out of his office, slamming the door in her wake.

She smiled for the first time in a very long time.

The business with the Crab immediately went well. They set up a base in the Meerkat's small flat. The kitchen was, unusually, the most significant room by far in the place – and her sanctuary. It contained a large, antique kitchen table filled with trays of growing lavender, an open island unit and rows and rows of cupboards filled with all the ingredients she'd collected on her travels over the years. The Crab arrived on their first day, dressed in a sparkling t-shirt and ripped jeans.

'Basic', she said to the Meerkat, assessing the room, 'but cosy', she added before the Meerkat could comment.

'Thanks', said the Meerkat, unsure if it was a compliment.

The Meerkat reached into the cupboard and pulled out two thick-rimmed trucker mugs.

'Remember these?' she laughed. 'Cup of tea or wine?' she asked.

'Jesus M, it's only 9am, we'd better go for the tea, or we will be in danger of getting nothing done', the Crab laughed. 'Maybe wine later? Ok, what's the plan?' The Crab asked.

'For the next few days we create a unique menu, we bake the menu and then taste it, did you bring your things so you can sleep over the next few nights? This is a lock-in. No leaving this flat till we have all the ideas in place', the Meerkat said. She needed to make this work; it was, after all, her only income.

'I'm all yours then, as long as your shower is working again?' The Crab said. 'I've been given permission to stay by his lordship who I think was secretly happy, because maybe I'd earn my own money through this, tight thing that he is.' She laughed loudly, and her enthusiasm filled the kitchen.

The Meerkat was keen to explore some new culinary adventure, something unique. 'Fritters of Elder-flower and lavender', 'Lavender, orange and gin' spread on shortbread hearts, and gin infused with rhubarb, fennel and star anise. She knew again after the first day, she'd met a kindred spirit with the Crab, her passion for all her ideas was infectious. On the second day, as they sipped tea at her kitchen table while the Meerkat assembled the ingredients for the latest cake experience, she explained to the Crab how she thought of her ideas.

'All cakes have stories', the Meerkat told the Crab, as she reached for a bowl off a high shelf. 'More than a flapjack or truffle, they connect us to our memories: of a lovely moment, celebrations, tradition, or of the people who made them for us. Before electric mixers and electric ovens, cakes were so difficult to make, they were the main measure of your accomplishments as a homemaker,' she said. 'You were considered a great mother if you could bake a cake.' She continued, tying her apron, 'there are stories of feminism, history, lovers and family all wrapped up in this lovely world of baking, people love it – look at Great British Bake Off!' the Meerkat laughed. She reached onto her high shelf and pulled down an old recipe book, a single torn out page fluttered to the floor.

'I can relate to that – what's lavender and vanilla cake?' the Crab laughed, picking up the page from the floor. It was an old, worn out recipe. 'Let's make it today.' The Meerkat frowned and took the recipe from the Crab and inspected it. She thought of her mother and her sister baking in the kitchen when she was young, the memories brought tears to her eyes. This was her sister's recipe.

'I love the idea of cake story-telling' the Crab said, brushing aside the Meerkat's emotional display. 'So much joy in it.' The Crab had the knack of getting the Meerkat into the now and out of her past. Maybe that's why she loved her, that's why their friendship was so special.

'Lavender cake, Lavender cake…' the Meerkat said as a tear ran down her eye, 'was a sort of sport…invented by my sister and eaten with a certain delightsome awe by all who knew its secret, which was after all a simple one – merely add a few sprigs of lavender into the bowl when you're mixing the cake, then pull it out before you bake it.' She sobbed lightly into her hands.

'Jesus M, it's time for wine, then let's bake that cake', the Crab exclaimed, slamming her hand on the table to jolt the Meerkat into action.

Lavender + Vanilla cake

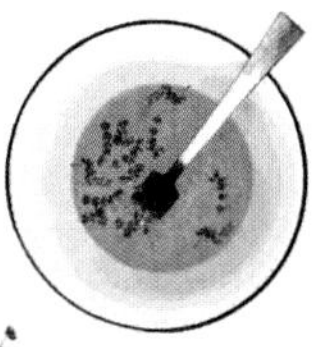

1 stick unsalted butter, softened

1 1/2 cups sugar

1 1/2 cups all-purpose flour

1/2 cup corn-starch

1 1/2 teaspoons baking powder

1/2 teaspoon kosher salt

1/2 cup milk

6 whites from large eggs, at room temperature

3 sprigs of lavender + vanilla extract, or more or less to taste (don't forget to take out the lavender before you put it into the oven.)

The Meerkat pulled all the ingredients down from her cupboards and plucked the lavender from one of the pots on her table. Seeing the ingredients laid out brought back precious, locked in memories.

She heated the oven to 350 degrees. She liberally added butter to a 10-inch, 12-cup tube pan. Then she sifted together the flour, corn-starch, baking powder and salt and set it aside. She measured the milk and added the sprig of lavender and set it to one side. She then creamed the softened butter with the sugar until it was fluffy by hand, mixing in the dry ingredients in three parts, alternating with the milk. The Crab whipped the egg whites to a stiff peak, and the Meerkat gently folded it into the cake batter with a lavender sprig, mixing thoroughly with her light, delicate hand. They both spooned out the mixture into the pan, smoothing the top. Then baked it for 30-35 minutes until the top was lightly browned and the edges were pulling away from the pan. Then the Meerkat liberally dusted it with powdered sugar and laid a piece of fresh lavender on the top.

When the cake was cooked, they both took a tentative forkful of the spongy cake. When the Meerkat's mouth closed in on it, it was like being back in her mum's kitchen with her sister years before.

She tentatively touched at the memory.

Over the next few days, the wall between the Crab and the Meerkat came down. Time stood still. The idea of the lavender became a central theme to inspire them. They made bottles of lavender, rose and vanilla extracts, they laughed and cried, when the nights drew in, they swapped the tea in the mugs for cheap wine. The Crab had stayed in her flat for a week, only leaving when she had a final ultimatum from the lordship (her husband).

Cakes with stories. Their idea was so unique, no one could get enough of it. They went from the cosy kitchen in the Meerkat's flat, to a lively open-plan restaurant in the city, in what seemed like minutes. Wedding contracts, events, posh dinner parties, their company grew and grew and grew and every deal they went for they won. Together they were on-fire, an unstoppable force. They settled into complementary roles, took on more and more young, energetic bakers who were keen to grow and shine. Food critics became friends and allies supporting their drive and growth, and the business took on a mind of its own. The press loved them, mini celebrities were being born. Podcasts, TV appearances, cookbooks. The Crab's charm and powers of persuasion were for once focused on an apparent goal. Male clients flocked around her, keen to gain attention and an invitation into her life. Soon, there was a second restaurant and then a third and fourth. From the outside, they looked like the picture of success.

'They are creating a monster', the Meerkat's mother said to the Crab's accountant at the launch of their fifth restaurant.

'It's making them, and everything around them money, but money can be ugly', the Crab's accountant stated in agreement.

'What can we do?' asked the Meerkat's mother.

'Very little', said the Crab's accountant with a sigh. He knew his determined client far too well.

'Intuition, not intellect, is the "open sesame" of yourself.'

Albert Einstein

The Meerkat was standing on the platform at Clapham Junction station. She was waiting for a train to take her to a big pitch for a contract that Devour so desperately needed to win. The Chameleon's number flashed up on her mobile. She hesitated. A wash of guilt spread over her, and she slid the answer button across the phone. She'd missed him. With a nervous excitement, she answered the call.

'Hello, M' he said. His voice sounded soft and feminine. Strange and distant.

It had been months since she'd last heard from him. Etched into her brain was their last night together – both crying, no one willing to talk.

'M', he tittered. The oddness in his voice just didn't make sense.

'M', he whispered, this time laughing in a feline voice. She tensed and could feel her nails pressing into the palm of her hands.

'It's me M, how are you?' he asked.

'I'm ok, it's so hectic at work, I'm sorry I didn't call to see how you were', she flushed, feeling an intense tug of guilt in the pit of her stomach. 'Is everything ok?'

'M, there is something I need to tell you before you find out.' he said and sighed into the phone. 'Maybe something I should have told you a long time ago.'

'What?', she asked. She felt a nervousness grow in her stomach. 'What is it?'

5

Timeline: Winter

In a black taxi, hurtling through the crowded, congested streets of London, the Meerkat was reading another text from the Chameleon.

'I'm so sorry, M' the text stated again.

She quickly flicked it off her screen and filed it under delete.

'Fuck him, her' she thought.

The confession had brought an avalanche of raw contact. The Chameleon wanted her approval, but she just couldn't stop feeling deeply hurt. In the taxi, driving down Burlington Street, they stopped at a red traffic light. Quite by chance, the Meerkat glanced up and noticed four massive posters in a large estate agent's window. The posters were larger than life. Her heart stopped. It was a poster with photos of the Bear. She stared in amazement. Hypnotised. Each photo was at a different angle, capturing his laughter, his serious face, his smile – each one reminded her of her time with him, intense and raw.

She found out much later that he'd modelled as a favour for a friend who works with a fancy estate agent. They had used his handsome, smiling face to sell expensive flats to funky, young people in the Docklands area. The intensity she felt when she saw the posters created a new type of panic in her mind. Unable to stop herself, she summoned up the courage to text the Bear:

TEXT: Are you about later? I'm in the middle of a business issue, and it would be great to get your advice?

TEXT: Sure, in Poland Street at the Lolo Bar, 7pm?

TEXT: Great, see you later...

She arrived five minutes late, expecting to see him leaning

at the bar. But, 10, 20, 25 minutes went by, and the Bear was no-where to be seen. She picked up her mobile and dialled the Elephant's number.

'How long should I wait?', the Meerkat asked. 'I'm thinking of leaving'. She noticed that she had an edge of desperation in her voice. 'I don't think he's going to come', she sighed. As she leant into the phone, she suddenly felt a tap on her back. She jumped in surprise.

'Now, why would you go and do that?' the Bear responded with a soft, gentle smile on his face.

'Sorry E, I've got to go, he's here'. She heard the Elephant laughing as she cut off the phone.

The Bear showed no visible sign of interest in her as he lounged back in a cosy, brown armchair that they have managed to grab. The conversation flowed – her life and success, the Crab, the Chameleon, the Elephant, it felt like a tiny world she'd been inhabiting. A tight circle of friends all fighting. He became more and more inquisitive and talkative. When she tried to talk about why she left home, he brushed it away and wouldn't listen.

'It's gone M, leave it alone'. he stated and ambled off to the bathroom.

They talked for hours. The intense passion she felt is so strong that it created a mild panic in her.

as she walks away later that night after kissing him twice on the cheek and jumping into a black cab alone back to her flat.

Bull

From Creaturepedia, the distinctively homemade (but well researched :) encyclopaedia

A Bull is more muscular and aggressive than the female of the species, the cow. The bull has long been an important symbol in many cultures.

Description

Bulls are capable of aggressive behaviour and require careful handling to ensure safety of humans and other animals. The need to move a bull in and out of its pen to cover cows exposes the handler to serious jeopardy of life and limb. Being trampled, jammed against a wall or gored by a bull was one of the most frequent causes of death of their handlers.

Warning:

The gentle bull, not the vicious one, most often kills or maims his keeper.

The Crab's marriage to the Stallion multi-millionaire ended bitterly due to an impromptu affair with a Bull. Her Stallion husband, relieved by all accounts, had built up an obsession with a young fowl, which by nature was much more manageable and complicit. The Meerkat had lost count of the affairs that the Crab had experienced since her marriage, but her relationship with the Bull had taken even her by surprise.

The Bull had an influence over the Crab that the Meerkat had never seen before. It happened so slowly, you could almost be forgiven for thinking it had been unplanned. But knowing him as she did now, everything he did was so carefully planned and crafted, right down to the smallest detail. She found out from the Crab, who was besotted with him, that he was incredibly gentle.

He was born to Nigerian parents in a London hospital. At three weeks old, he was given up to a white, working-class family in Salford in the hope that he would have a better life. His foster parents had at least twelve African children, including the Bull, living in their house and money was tight. At fourteen he fell in with the local gang and became so violent that he was sent away to boarding school by the state. His further isolation contributed more to his aggression. Then he made his first friend. His English teacher. Rather than commit suicide, which was always on his mind, he was encouraged to study. It was then that he and everyone around him realised that he was exceptionally gifted. His life quickly turned around. Following his top grades at school, he went to a top university in London and got a first in Law. He then grew into a natural hustler, never getting fed up with wealth acquisition. He was domineering and demanding. The Crab used to shrink a little around him: he detested her 'ego', so she had to adapt.

One day, the Bull just charged into Devour. The Meerkat was busy in the kitchen, but she couldn't help but notice his presence and the strange effect he had on the Crab. Then the Meerkat noticed that he'd started eating there every day and sitting in front of the bar. The Crab would scurry around when he came in, making sure he had the best service and food. The final realisation came for the Meerkat that he was here to stay when he paraded around their restaurant, welcoming all of their guests. Why didn't she like him? The Meerkat weighed this up daily, and every day a new reason arose.

He didn't have a neck.

His bulky, muscular shoulders just went straight up into his head.

He snorted when laughing.

He had large, plump hands that he waved when he shouted, which was often.

He charmed everyone around him.

He was a force of nature in any room (not always in a good way)

But more recently she had noticed he always licked his lips as he walked past one of their beautiful French waitresses. His laces were always conveniently coming undone at the point he walked by. She'd watched his beady black eyes flick sideways to see who was around and then glance hungrily down her top at her breasts.

She was amazed at how much she could loathe someone.

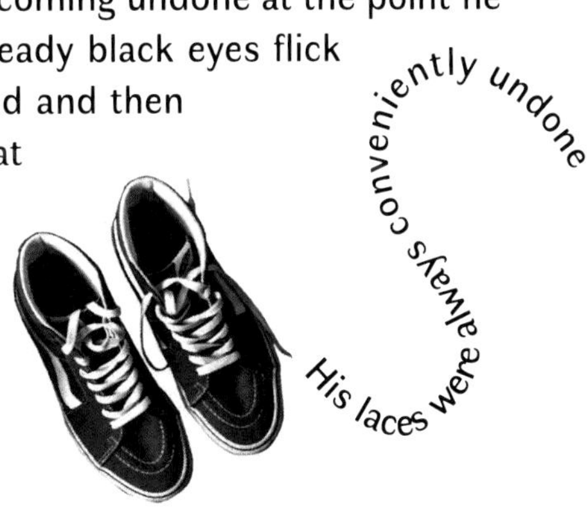

6

Timeline: Autumn

The Bear texted unexpectedly. It had been months since she last saw him. Her life had gathered into a non-urgent pace.

Text: Do you fancy a night out? Bear

She wanted to say no. She liked him too much, and she was pretty sure it was one-sided. But, like us all, she sought happiness and his text gave her a glimmer of hope.

Text: Ok. M

Text: A little bar called Trailer Happy in Notting Hill on Wednesday at 7pm? B

Text: Great, see you there. M

The bar stood out in her mind as fun, but intimate. The fun bit she craved. The intimate bit filled her with worry. Wednesday night arrived slowly. She was early again, even though she tried to be late. No Bear. She soaked up the fun, intoxicating atmosphere that surrounded her. Coloured Toby jugs all lined the bar with different famous faces, every one of them laughing at her. The Bear arrived down the stairs fifteen minutes later. Quiet and strong.

'Cutting it fine', he laughed.

'Mm, I'd say late', she smiled back at him, wishing she hadn't arrived so early and looked so obviously keen.

'How's the strange life of the Meerkat?' The Bear asked.

It was the most complicated question he could ask, so she just laughed and let him talk. He ordered one large cocktail for them both to share. A 'volcano cocktail', it stood out on the menu as one of the Trailer Happy specials. A communal volcano-shaped bowl arrived shortly after, with blue, south sea images carved into its side. They sipped from long straws to avoid getting singed by the flaming crater at the centre of the bowl. It tasted like an innocent mango smoothie. The drink and the scent of the Bear. She'd not tasted this type of feeling for so long, she soaked it up.

'More volcano?', he suggested when they had too quickly finished the first one.

'Yes,' she nodded and laughed. A new flaming volcano cocktail arrived. She sipped at it hungrily.

'Why did you leave and never come back?' he asked, suddenly pensive.

She gulped on her cocktail. It was a story she'd rehearsed over in her mind again and again and here was her chance to explain. Then, it was like a wave had crashed over her. She lost the ability to talk, move or even signal for help. She could hear the Bear trying to speak to her, but it was like she'd fallen down a deep well and couldn't understand or speak. With her limited communication skills, which involved a series of moans and grunts, he struggled to make sense of her words. Her brain was moving, but her mouth couldn't function. He eventually carried her into a taxi after she lost her ability to move any parts of her body. Their taxi ride home was conducted in silence. He dropped her off at her flat, and the taxi drove away into the night. She just caught the Bear saying to the taxis driver before they pulled away:

'Jesus, she was like a zombie.' He spoke with disbelief in his voice.

She crawled up her flat stairs, barely aware of where she was. When she woke up the next day, she cringed with the shame of it, 'A zombie.'

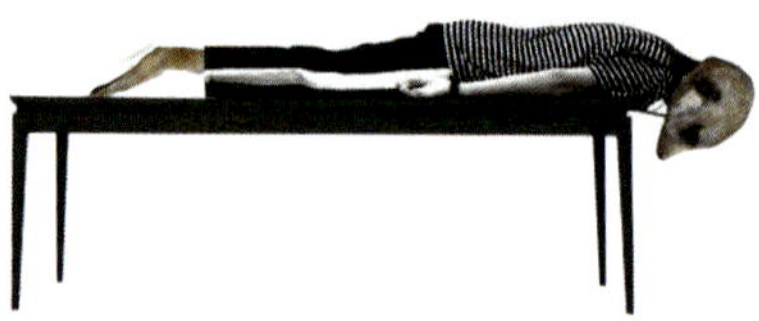

As Devour grew, the Meerkat's love of food withered. The board and management looked to her to drive forward new ideas for the future of the whole business, while their staff needed constant guidance, direction and inspiration. The day-to-day reality of running the business, meanwhile, meant that most days she found herself dealing with all the nitty-gritty: baking was so far from her every-day life.

The press couldn't get enough of Devour – their latest recipe, their new book, the new restaurant openings. She had a brief look at this moment of fame. It was not her world. But the worst thing was the Crab. Every step that the Meerkat made that was successful was becoming more deeply resented by the Crab. Glory and wealth was the Crab's world and hers only. Then one day, the Meerkat realised she was no longer in a partnership or a two-sided thing. She was in a neat triangle. The Bull, the Crab and the Meerkat.

All too soon an unspoken competition.

So shiny on the outside. On the inside, everything was relentless, exhausting and fast-paced. No one was the winner. Resentment and anger boiled away, ready to explode. For the first time ever, the Meerkat started dreading any time she found herself alone with the Crab. It always ended in shouting accusations about who was putting in the most effort and time. The success they were having in setting up and running the business just didn't translate back into the joy they should both feel. They hardly talked anymore. The red ribbons that once bound them together so tightly grew black, fraying and were flapping in the wind. Their unspoken conflict rippled across the business like a cancer. When the Meerkat mentioned it to the Elephant, she merely told her about her theory on money and power. She was not surprised by their conflict, in fact, she was amazed they had got as far as they had.

'The theory that money + power = success:
It's strange that when we only live 30,000 days in our lifetime that the fight and drive for power and money seems to take up a hell of a lot of people's time.

The more money you have, the more power you wield over people, the more successful people deem you. Money magnifies your most prominent personality trait, for example, if you're generous you become more generous, if you're greedy you become greedier, enough is never enough. The irony of it is, when people are on their death bed, they never lie there and wish they had more money'

'Love is the absence of judgement.'

Dalai Lama

Everything was relentless. Devouring her daily.

'M, you are going to wake up at forty with no children, no husband and time will have passed you by. All in the pursuit of what?' Her father asked her with concern one afternoon in an unprompted phone call.

'Oh Dad, stop worrying' the Meerkat said. The Bear's memory flashed in her mind.

'Come on, be brave, there must be someone,' he replied.

'When will you stop worrying about me?' The Meerkat said.

'Never', he sighed 'You are all we've got M.' They both knew it was her sister's birthday, but it was carefully not mentioned; she could hear him softly sob in the background. She couldn't bear to hear him cry. She couldn't remember the last time he smiled, and that thought pulled at her heart.

'I'll try', she said.

'Life's too short M', he managed to say, before he put down the phone.

7

Outside the restaurant window a cloud shifted, the sunlight fell onto the Meerkat's face, reminding her that there was life outside. Her father was right, she knew that in her heart. With a bold determination one day, she woke up and decided to book time off. She'd always been in love with Italy. Its vast countryside, the beautiful old buildings, its delicious food – and she'd heard a rumour the Bear was there.

When she arrived a week later, she spent her days exploring. Walking through the streets, following around tour guides, listening to the history of the city. Hundreds of little islands with interconnected canals, bridges and walkways. Over the years they had added extra land to the city with man-made extensions constructed from marble and wooden planks, then they carefully built new buildings. No two single structures were the same. Bright canary yellow, dusky pink, mint green, light purple –an explosion of colours and textures.

Standing on the sidewalk, she loved the way the sea had reclaimed the lower level of the buildings, submerging the grand main doors of the houses half underwater. She delighted at the way every beautiful, old, worn out door had a little exclusive landing deck for visiting boats. You could get lost in the streets of Venice. This idea seemed like pure luxury to her. On the first few days of her visit, she allowed herself to think of the Bear. He created a calm in her mind. She foolishly found herself looking for him around every corner. His memory was fixed in her mind. It was strange that even though she was surrounded by thousands of tourists, she still felt very alone.

On the last night of her holiday, having spent a long time deciding what to wear, she looked in the mirror. Her hair had grown longer, and her natural curls had exploded into rippling waves flowing down her shoulders, wild and carefree. The lines and dark shadows under her eyes had gone, replaced by a soft, smooth glow. As she walked out into the city to explore its beauty for the last time, she felt happy. If not a little alone. Wandering through the streets, she discovered a small restaurant hidden in a secret stone-clad mews, the reviews were that the food was outstanding. The roof of the restaurant had long since collapsed, leaving nature to reclaim the space. Ivy, moss and wildflowers burst in colour all around the walls. It was a place of serenity and beauty. She ordered from the menu and started reading her book. The artistry of the space settled her creative mind. As the Meerkat arched down to look at her book, from the corner of her eye, she caught sight of a beautiful, exquisite individual, with long, blonde hair and tanned, elongated legs. She was laughing at a bulky man with curly black hair. He had his back to the Meerkat, so she couldn't quite see his face.

The beautiful female lightly touched his hand, kissed his cheek twice and then seductively walked out of sight, looking back over her shoulder several times as she strode away. He gently waved in her direction, and the Meerkat could hear him laughing at her smiles. The Meerkat quickly turned away, afraid to be caught watching and looked down at her book. The book was about trees, the nature of the eco-system of trees. She didn't realise they communicated with each other, protected each other and one on its own was lonely – they needed a forest to survive. It made sense.

'Hello,' a voice suddenly said, leaning over her table, casting a huge shadow. 'Who is this curious individual and what is she doing in my part of the world?' He padded her arm and looked into her wide eyes. She looked up, and everything stopped. He was wearing a crisp, white shirt that was hiding his unruly hair.

'Hello,' she said, as she took a sharp intake of breath.

'May I?' he said, pointing to the seat opposite. She waved her arm casually in its direction and welcomed him back into her world.

'So, how's life? The Bear laughed. 'The last time I saw you, you couldn't speak. You were crawling up your flat stairs after that mango cocktail you decided to down as quickly as possible.' He laughed again. He acted out the scrabbling act she must have done when stumbling up the stairs with his paws.

She cringed and inwardly drew a sharp breath that brought back memories of that night so brightly in her mind and flushed. She had played that dreadful night over and over again in her imagination, but her mind had refused to remember much of it. Leaving her with new gaps, confused visions and shame. What did she do? He never called her again, so she had presumed it was embarrassing. As if reading her thoughts...

'It wasn't that bad', said the Bear, the smile on his face broadening. 'I've never been on a date where a woman starts every single topic of conversation, and I've also never met someone who could talk so much, minutes before losing the ability to stand or speak!' He laughed so hard at the memory, tears welled up in his eyes.

'I'm sorry I left home without saying goodbye', the Meerkat said, suddenly flushed a blushing red from her chest up to her face. 'I had to go, then when I left, going back became an impossible thing', she said.

He paused. 'M, let's not go there tonight', he said, almost to himself in a whisper.

When dinner was over, she found him by her side as they wandered the streets of Venice. Their hands brushed together a few times and then she found herself holding his hand. It buried her tiny delicate hand in its hold. They arrived at a light blue building with a large balcony and stood outside, waiting. Waiting for what, she wasn't sure. He then pulled out a small key and struggled with his large hands to twist it in the ancient wooden door. Swearing with frustration, he pushed the door hard and disappeared inside. She followed him into the low-lit hallway. She felt his hand reach for her arm. He suddenly pulled her close and smothered her with hard passionate kisses. Much later, when they wrapped themselves around each other naked, his smell and the feel of his hair filled her with a feeling of lust and anticipation. One that she hadn't felt for years.

So that's what they are all saying she thought. Her anger built. Her resentments simmered. *Is that what the Bear thinks?* When she asked him about it later that night, he laughed at the madness of the comment.

'Be brave little M, don't worry so much', the Bear told her, stroking her face.

She learneds to block it out, put on a front. A phase of her life erased and forgotten. There was just no way to rationalise it, so she didn't.

'Love is the absence of judgement.'

Dalai Lama

Falling in love is one scary, emotional rollercoaster. Only the brave or naive fall in love. Those that have been hurt in love before will at no cost allow the ribbons to tightly attach again to another's heart until that love is either forgotten or gut-wrenching loneliness drives them into another's warm arms.

The Bear was a contradiction. A bi-polar Bear. On the one side, he had a quick-paced, black sense of humour that was magnetic and compelling. No self-editing, just confident, fast, brilliant observations on other animals, his habitat or himself. This side of the bear drew her in, yet half scared her to death. It was like a drug that she was growing to depend on for her energy, happiness and comfort. She'd never needed this from anyone before, and while it was strangely alluring, it was also incredibly frightening to feel such a connection. A loss of control and a need for another. Love made her feel vulnerable, scared and yet anchored. What would she do without him, her mind would repeatedly ask her. As bright and compelling as his funny side was, there was an alternative side which was a total contradiction that she worried about. Two compelling sides to his deep personality, both showing themselves at different stages and interludes. His other side was dark. It was a deep self-loathing of himself and his faults.

'I'm lazy', he would invariably say. Despite his 10am-8pm working hours.

He wanted to just hibernate. To snuggle down into bed for the winter and wake up when the first leaves appeared on the trees. But commercial life doesn't work in seasons. So, on dark, cold winter mornings, he would struggle to get out of bed.

Everybody has two sides to their nature: some, like the Bear were more extreme, but his was well hidden. When she grew to know him more, she came to realise that both sides were an integral part of his nature. His dark side brought with it a self-scanning process. A review of events gone by. The time he spent in that self-loathing, guilty state made him think more about his true nature, which resulted as time went by in a more empathic

9

'The people who really care won't hurt you. But if they do, you'll see it in their eyes, for they will be hurting too.'

Anon

Timeline: Winter

The Bear and the Jackal. A night out. Just a fun drink. 'I need to go M, he told her, I've not seen him for ages.' She'd missed him, the house felt alone without his presence.

'M', the Bear shouted as he rushed up the stairs later that night. The door slammed open with such a force that she jumped out of bed and ran to the landing, thinking he was hurt.

'Why the FUCK didn't you tell me about you and the Jackal?' he shouted. 'You've known all along. You've drip-fed me information and told me half-truths.' He looked at her with new, cold eyes that she'd never seen before.

The Bear had assumed that the relationship with the Jackal ended when they were eighteen. What he didn't know until that night was that in the previous few years, the Meerkat and the Jackal had been together again. The Bear couldn't understand at the time why the Jackal had been so opposed to their relationship, but now he knew. It all added up. The Jackal had been jealous and wanted her for himself. Not to keep, but to endlessly play with. It was not that she had been unfaithful to the Bear, there was no overlap this time, she only had eyes for the Bear, but that didn't matter to him.

'What, what, what has he said?' she stammered in despair.

'You know what the Jackal said to me?' the Bear played out the scene word for word, scoffing as he said it. 'He asked me, "So, did you have an affair with the Meerkat when she was still with the Chameleon? Was it because of you that she left him?"

"Sorry Jackal", I said to him, "With me? What are you trying to say? That I've somehow taken the Meerkat off the Chameleon and broken up their engagement?"

"Well yes", the Jackal said.' The Bear paused and looked directly at the Meerkat's distorted face. She was sitting on the stairs, sinking more and more into the soft carpet with every word that he spoke.

'As I looked at my brother in the eye, something snapped in my mind, and I knew. I knew. Don't you mean she had an affair with you? I asked him. Suddenly I was aware of the game, I bet you were both laughing at me' he growled. 'What the hell happened?' he barked at her. 'How dare he accuse me of having an affair with you behind the Chameleon's back when all along it had been him!'

'The part that gets me', said the Bear, 'was he knew I was so happy, he just didn't give a shit'. His eyes were stony.

(The Bear's birthday, many years before)

In her crazy drunken state, when the Meerkat had fallen down the stairs at the Bear's birthday after she'd watched him kiss the female with the fantastic boobs, she'd been captured by the Jackal. The Jackal, watching her anguish, sensing her loneliness and vulnerability, had crept up and taken her sensibility. It was something she had almost denied to herself. The Jackal was charming. Charismatic. Intense. After that night, when he told her his supposedly true feelings, she had started to feel wanted again. A tiny seed of doubt still grew in her mind. She ignored it.

From the loneliness of the relationship with the Chameleon, she'd found a new intensity in life. It was unexpected and unbelievable. He had been waiting carefully in the background, to devour her when she let down her guard. Once he had her affections, the narcissistic, self-centred male appeared again. Her ignorance proved catastrophic. But without this knowledge, she invited him into her habitat, and a new game had begun. The game was a form of cat and mouse. This game, she knew from old times, was his favourite pastime.

The thrill to him was only in the chase...

He would chase her, charm her and then say it was over and let her go. When he had pinned her down, and she was under his control, he would quickly lose interest. She would wait. Cry. Wait. Convince herself it was all over. Then he would turn up on her doorstep with a glint in his eye, filled with lust and passion. When he left, he would go back to his old life like nothing had happened. He could lie with such incredible ease. *He would lie even when the truth would do.* Fancy nightclubs, crazy nights out, fuelled with cocktails and drugs. The darker life of their illicit affair. She would meet him in far-flung trendy places, feeling exotically excited before they met, but when she left their times together, she'd feel emptier than when she'd arrived. He drained her energy, her youth and her happiness, using it up to make himself feel more powerful, young and needed. How can someone say so much when actually they mean so little? It was a crazy game that would have gone on forever if she hadn't grown sick and tired of feeling sick and tired. It left her mentally bruised, battered and humiliated. She'd never allowed herself to be played with like this before.

One day, everything changed. Her friend the Otter, unsuspecting of their affair, innocently told her how much the Jackal was in love with his wife, the Raven. The Meerkat didn't want to know or ask, but she did.

'How do you know he loves his wife, I thought they had split up and he wasn't happy?' she stammered, trying to keep an element of control in her voice. Ironically, the Meerkat was still nursing a hangover from another wild, passionate, madness-filled night with the Jackal. Feeling wretched and sick to the stomach, she waited for his reply.

'Split up, oh, haven't you heard,' the Otter clapped his hands with glee, 'what an amazing husband he is?' He laughed and patted her hand. 'The Jackal took the Raven away last weekend for their anniversary to an incredible, five-star hotel in Rome,' he said. 'You know, one of those places where you can choose your own pillows with different scents and firmness. As a gift, he had specially flown in from a famous Italian designer, handmade Italian ballet shoes in red with her name embroidered on the side. You know she used to be a dancer?' He paused to make sure she was listening.

'No' she said in a whisper.

'According to the rumours, the Jackal spent hours in shops finding all their old songs on records. The ones they used to listen to when they first got together and presented them to her with an old record player.' The Otter clapped his hands in delight. The ability of someone to lie in such detail.

When she challenged the Jackal days later, he'd paused to reply as if he knew he'd been caught at his own game.

'Does it matter, little M?' He laughed and then laughed harder when he saw her tears.

10

Timeline: Winter

Her unforgivable mistake. After the full confession, the Bear had stormed out of the flat, loaded down with all of his things. She wept and asked him to stay, but he shrugged and walked out of the door in disgust. She had some news she wanted to tell him when he got home that night, but she hadn't had the chance. Something unexpected had happened. A baby was growing inside of her, unaware of all of this conflict. But, instead of telling him, she whirled into an endless spiral of despair as he slammed the door in her face. Christmas day was spent in bed feeling like death had arrived at her door.

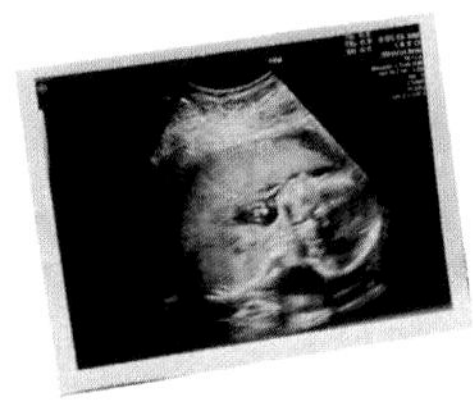

'Our prime purpose in life is to help others and if you can't help them, at least don't hurt them.'

Dalai Lama

'I've tried, but I can no longer take it. Your life's too dramatic. You take too much,' the Bear told her the following week on a phone call to ask when he could collect the last of his belongings.

'Can we still be friends?' she asked, both devastation and desperation in her voice.

'Of course, I'm not going anywhere. But I need some space', he whispered down the phone.

Heartbroken. They exchanged belongings, friends picked sides, and everyone moved on. She wanted to die. Honestly and sincerely, it felt like death. She had spent almost every waking minute with him for months. Same life. Same bed. Shared jokes. Kisses, memories, good and bad times. He was kind, sincere, honest, and SHE had torn him down. SHE HAD DESTROYED HIS TRUST. Now, she just wanted him back. She wanted their life back.

She went to the gym

Tried to focus on new menus

Picked at her food

Walked to the bus

She just felt empty and lost.

All broken and alone.

The practicalities of being pregnant were ignored. She couldn't even think of carrying his baby alone. The loss of the Bear was too substantial to bear.

No twelve-week scan photo to coo over with her family and friends. No twenty-week scan to look at and see its small fingers with tiny nails, perfectly formed. The baby kept growing. One morning, she woke up and could start to feel its little fists hitting her stomach wall, like small explosions of popcorn. It had woken up and had started a life of its own. Unaware of her thoughts and her heartbreak. Growing quietly in the comfort of her womb. No-one knew it existed. She hid it from her parents, batting away their calls, saying she was too busy at Devour.

One Sunday afternoon her mum turned up uninvited into her flat. Her curtains were still drawn at 2pm, and she still had on her baggy pyjamas. Her mother had argued with the Meerkat's dad that very morning: she told the Meerkat later about their exchange.

'I'm worried about M', her mother had said to the Meerkat's father. She had no singing tone in her voice anymore. The singing tone had died many years before, with her sister.

'Keep out', her father had said. 'She'll be ok, she doesn't want us interfering in her life. She's a grown woman', he sighed.

'Something's not right', her mother had replied. 'She's my child, she will always be my child, I know something's not right,' she'd said flatly and wouldn't be reassured.

Her mother then insisted they jump onto the train that very day, undeterred. She knew something was wrong. When the Meerkat's parents arrived at her flat, her mother didn't wait to be invited in. Instead, she rushed in and flitted around the flat like a mad moth. All in a quick haze. Taking everything in. Soaking in the atmosphere, the objects, the smells and the sounds. Her father had stood awkwardly by the door, sensing the worry.

'Where's the Bear? Where are all of his things? What's happened?' her mother asked in a panic.

When she looked into her daughter's eyes. the realisation of the pain she was going through hit her hard. Her mother knew. It now all added up.

'God, I don't want to hurt like this anymore', the Meerkat cried to her mother that night. Her mother had pulled her close and held her like she did when she was a baby, stroking her head and humming a sad song. The first song she'd heard her mother sing for years.

Morning came slowly. The Meerkat's nights had been dark and alone until this one.

'Take a shower and get changed M, we need to talk', her mother had said. 'Then we need to go and see the doctor about this baby.'

The Meerkat looked at her in surprise.

'Resentment is like drinking poison and waiting for someone to die.'

Buddha

The Meerkat was sure that the Crab could feel her devastation. Even if she did, she did nothing to acknowledge it. Instead, they occasionally nodded at each other across the opposite ends of the restaurant. Nothing was natural or joyful. The Meerkat, conscious of her crime, was struggling to hide her bump in big baggy dresses and large woollen jumpers. The Crab had been eyeing her suspiciously for weeks. She'd ignored her swollen eyes, her thin, gaunt face, but the growing bump had caught her attention.

'M, are you pregnant?' She asked, marching into the restaurant one day.

The Meerkat's eye's brimmed with tears, and that was all the Crab needed to know.

'We are on the verge of a major deal to open our seventh restaurant, seriously?' The Crab was blindly furious. A wave of simmering anger flashed across her face, her resentment was so acute that it was like a thick aura wrapping around her in a black haze. The Crab then turned around sharply and slammed the door behind her. Everyone in the restaurant looked up as the loud crack of the door shuddered in the frame.

'C, I didn't mean this to happen!' the Meerkat shouted after her.

As the Meerkat's stomach grew so did the Crab's sense of injustice, and every ounce of it was channelled towards her.

As the weeks rolled by and the pain didn't fade, the Meerkat realised one major thing; she'd thought she would spend the rest of her life with the Bear. Then, the day when their relationship ended so suddenly and dramatically, the future she envisioned for herself fell apart, along with her sense of self-worth and identity. She spiralled into depression, broke out into panic attacks, and had thoughts of suicide. The baby, although largely ignored, had started to tap the inside of her tummy with its tiny, delicate fingers. Its rhythm kept her alive. 'I'm here', it was trying to tell her. On some nights, she would wake up and forget the Bear was gone and reach for his hand and then the cruel realisation would hit her again and again. 'Just get over it', her friends would say, 'just move on'. Hearing their words would only deepen her shame. While this might work in the corporate world, it didn't work with matters of the heart. There was no magic button to press.

The Meerkat heard the Raven before she saw her. The curtains at the entrance to the restaurant were made of blued eyelets, and they hung down and across the floorboards, fanning themselves out like wedding trains. The Raven ripped open the curtains and gestured towards the waitress, who pointed in the Meerkat's direction.

The Meerkat's light peach lipstick tasted like ash in her mouth.

'DO ME A FAVOUR?' The Raven shouted across from the middle of the restaurant, 'JUST HELP ME WITH A THING I NEED TO KNOW'. The Spring sun was behind her, filtering through the diamonds hanging from around her neck and bouncing off in little trails of light. Like a sniper taking aim.

'Of-course', the Meerkat sighed.

'Quite frankly, I've started to hear you're one of many. But I also hear that there is a baby involved', she coughed to blink the flash of tears from her eyes, 'Just so you're clear, me and daddy are not tolerating this. You are clearly trying to trap him with this thing', she said, pointing at the Meerkat's stomach. 'I'm going to get our lawyers involved', she said.

The Crab appeared from nowhere. The Meerkat could see it in her face: the sharp sideways glance, the fast flaring of the nostrils, the anger flushing her cheeks and nearly boiling over.

'You know, I don't think that's a good idea to make unfounded accusations', the Crab said, 'that husband of yours takes too many liberties.'

The Raven moved towards her, a bright, diamond covered handbag tightly grasped in her hand. With a ruffle of feathers from the cloak around her shoulders, she raised her hand. The Crab's face froze. At that moment, the Raven slapped the Crab hard across the face. A sharp, cracking sound filled the room. The Crab took a step back.

'Darling, you need to learn how to control that dog of yours,' the Crab laughed.

'My lawyer will be in touch', the Raven crowed. She then glanced at the Meerkat and strode out.

Everyone in the restaurant had followed the scene. Faces were peering at them, wondering what was going to happen next. Better than any Netflix movie, this was action in real life. The Meerkat stood blushing, ashamed and belittled. The Crab looked at her for a full ten seconds in amazement. The Meerkat stayed silent.

'Don't mention it', She said to the Meerkat as she marched away.

Liverpool Street tube platform was ram-packed with commuters. All were filled with an apocalyptic sense of urgency to get home. As the Meerkat pushed her way into the throng, her feet ached, she was exhausted and her stomach swelled. It was expanding hard against her tight, white, crisply-ironed blouse. Still alien to her, she didn't think to protect it. A tube slid into the platform. Two women beside her nudged their way on. Pushing their way in regardless of the lack of space. Pressing against each other in an uncomfortable silence. Then the tube raced through the endless dark tunnels, the hot carriages airless. Everyone was trapped tightly against each other in an uncomfortably short distance.

'Hello,' a deep frown crossed the woman's face as she looked down at the Meerkat's stomach. It was a familiar face, but the Meerkat could not calibrate where it was from. Inches apart, they look into each other's eyes.

'Hello', the Meerkat tentatively ventured, with a questioning tone in her voice. *Who is she*? she thought. Her brain was so tired she couldn't function.

'IT'S ME M!', the female started raising her voice to an uncomfortable volume, as if the Meerkat had a problem with her hearing. *She knows my name,* the Meerkat thought, *who is she?*

Then the Meerkat paused. Space and time stood still. Her mind flashed back to intimate moments, soft kisses, fingers entwined. It felt like a different life, one that she'd left so far behind her and kept hidden deep in her memory. Past and present images flashed around her head, playing tricks with her eyes and her mind.

'My God' the Meerkat gasped. The remarkable eyes, the mouth, the smile.

'How are you M? I've missed you so much', the Chameleon said, more softly this time. 'How are you, my love?' the Chameleon whispered.

The Meerkat angled her head, straining to listen and understand. The Chameleon had always had beautiful, black wavy hair. She'd grown it long to create a more feminine look, soft, long curls with new energy bounced around her face. She was wearing dark blue eye makeup, bright red lipstick and heavy clotted foundation that was pitted around her stubble. She was wearing a white, cotton blouse that was so tight it bulged open at the buttons around her new, hormone-induced breasts, threatening to pop open at any minute. Her black skirt was uncomfortably short. She wore strange, high black heels with a thick strap across her ankle. As the Meerkat looked down, she realised that they had on the same outfit. A white shirt with a black skirt and black shoes.

'Not looking so great M, tell me, are you married now?' the Chameleon asked.

'No', the Meerkat replied.

'Sorry', the Chameleon said. She read the sadness in the Meerkat's emaciated face.

'I'm sorry too, Cam', the Meerkat sighed. 'Everything is so different for me now'. The Chameleon looked down at her swollen, pregnant belly and looked up in hurt and disgust.

'Congratulations', the Chameleon stated in a mocking tone. 'Who's the lucky male?' she scoffed.

'I'm on my own with this', the Meerkat sniffed and brushed the tears from her eyes.

'I'm here,' the Chameleon whispered. 'I'm always here, M, I've always been here.' The acute feeling of loss the Chameleon was feeling was making her brave. Standing so close to the Meerkat but so far away from being able to touch her, the Chameleon looked in turmoil.

'Could you love me again?' the Chameleon asked outright.

'Could you love me as a woman, I could help, does it matter what gender I am?' the Chameleon said. Her mournful eyes filled with tears.

'So much has changed,' the Meerkat said with a sigh. 'So much'.

The tight space they first found themselves in seemed to have grown as the crowd near them pulled back and created a small, clear circle of space around them. Shifty looks and tight, grinning faces strain to listen intently to their conversation while trying to look like they hadn't even noticed what was happening around them. The more the Meerkat and the Chameleon raced through the tunnels, the more frustrated the Chameleon got.

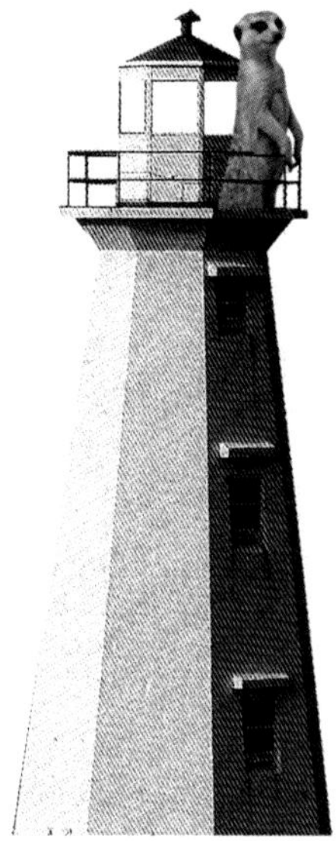

'I have to say', the Chameleon started to say quietly but then built up in volume. 'YOU'RE A LIGHTHOUSE M', she said. From the frown on her face, she was remembering what they had lost and how much it hurt.

'A lighthouse?' The Meerkat said, looking back at her with a questioning, puzzled look.

'YES! You're a person who shines so brightly on another person at one brief moment in their life and then moves on as quickly, leaving them in darkness, lost and BEWILDERED', the Chameleon said.

The tube grew quieter as everyone stared in their direction. All looking at the small, dishevelled, pregnant female and the tall female who so obviously was once a male. As the tube door opened at the next station, five stations from her final destination, the Meerkat instinctively made a break for the door. Bursting and pushing through the crowds of people. Desperate for air. Just as the tube doors closed, she glanced back. She could still hear the Chameleon shouting and waving her arms so wildly that her tight, white shirt stretched across her chest and threatened to burst open by the strain of the gesticulating movement.

'RUN AWAY M, THAT'S WHAT YOU ALWAYS DO!' The Chameleon shouted. 'WHEN THINGS GET TOUGH, YOU RUN AWAY' she yelled.

The Meerkat escaped from the platform, running hard up the escalators into the chilly London air. Panting and holding her stomach, she leaned over and retched onto the pavement. Wave after wave of vomit, the sick repeatedly splashed up against a shop window. When she managed to catch her breath, she scrabbled in her bag for her phone and in her panic, she phoned the Crab. The Crab, after she related the story, shouted three short words above the noise of the traffic and then cut off the call.

'CALL THE SAMARITANS.'

There was a sudden, profound, intense realisation that hit her so hard she lost her breath. She had no friend in the Crab anymore. Her world had just got smaller, as the three people she thought most cared for her had shut her out.

'Our unconscious drives us and dominates.'

Gerald Zaltman

Standing on the busy London pavement after calling the Crab, it suddenly started to rain. It began in little drips and then it came down in sheets, lashing against her body, sticking her hair to her face. A passing bus stopped in front of her, and she instinctively climbed on. Where would she go? she wondered. Her flat was so lonely. Its emptiness filled her with dread every time she walked in the door. Everything she touched reminded her of the Bear. She sat down on a seat in the bus and sobbed into her folded, outstretched arms and started stroking her stomach. Something she did more and more subconsciously. The stroke of her hand comforted her soul and the tiny baby sleeping and almost forgotten within.

'Are you ok, can I help love?' A beautiful, very ancient old female Owl in front of her offered her a tissue, brushing against the Meerkat's bulging stomach with her delicate hand. 'Nothing is worth that many tears, look at how blessed you are love', the Owl said, as she made a curved sign with her hand.

'Come and sit over here love', the Owl said, patting the seat beside her. The Owl removed her white stick and a large, brown book from the seat to make way for the Meerkat. She patted the chair. She placed the stick to one side and moved the book onto her lap and stroked it wistfully with her delicate, light, feathery hands. 'My life', she said, stroking the book with a shrug of her shoulders. The Owl's face was feathered with fine wrinkles, her bright brown eyes were covered in cloudy white cataracts. Her hands were like tissue, light and delicate.

'Your life?' asked the Meerkat.

'Yes, my love', the Owl said, her voice just a whisper above the noise of the bus engine.

'My life, it's all in here' she said, patting the book, smiling contently.

The Owl opened the book and stroked the first page. 'Me as a small girl with my sister and my mother and father', she said her face calm and happy. The Meerkat didn't think the Owl could see the black and white photo through her cloudy cataracts. The photo showed two small girls playing on a beach next to their parents, lying on a black and white checked blanket, smiling and laughing. The memories were filling up the Owl's mind, and she smiled. 'She was beautiful my mother, kind and gentle – just like my sister. My sister died last year, cancer. She was so brave, but it got her in the end'. The Meerkat looked at the two smiling, beautiful girls in the photo, both with feathery hair streaming down their shoulders. The Owl slowly and wistfully turned over the page.

'This is my love, Bee and me', the Owl said, stroking the photo of a tall, handsome male. He was standing next to a young, beautiful Owl holding her hand. 'He's been gone fifteen years this year', she paused. 'Bowel cancer.' Her face twisted in the pain of the memory so crisp and so clear in her mind. 'We found it too late. We had fifty years of marriage though, before that. A lovely life, he was a remarkable creature – how he made me laugh,' the Owl said with a giggle.

'Any grandchildren?' the Meerkat asked.

'I've got twelve', the Owl answered with a smile, 'and two great-grandchildren.'

'Twelve', said the Meerkat. 'Yes, me and Bee had two sons and two daughters, our house was filled with kids when they were growing up, the best years of my life – not like these days, our house is so quiet' she smiled, this time filled with a little sadness. The Meerkat reached for her hand and stroked it. A delicate tissue hand, filled with light bones. The Owl flipped over the page. 'Me and our first little Bee' the Owl said, showing the Meerkat a photo of a baby with feathery black hair and a bright-yellow face – 'he had jaundice when he was born', she laughed, 'his crying nearly drove us all mad!'

'He's beautiful', the Meerkat said.

'He's a busy Bee these days', the Owl said. 'A top barrister in London you know, he sometimes struggles to see his old mum. But he's always there when I need him. He's retiring this year, or so he tells me. Then he says, we will have much more time together.' She smiled. 'The thing is love, between me and you, I'm not sure how long I've got' she said, still smiling. 'I feel like my Bee is calling me, I miss him so much, it's time we were together again. Life goes so quickly love, don't waste it,' the Owl said. 'No regrets from me though – I'm nearly at the end of my life story, the final chapter, and what a life I've lived.' She smiled again, patting the book, her face lit up with the memories. The bus drew into the next stop. 'This is me Jim,' the Owl softly shouted to the bus driver, grabbing her white stick and pushing the brown book into an old Tesco's bag.

'No problem', the driver shouted back. The old, worn out, aging Badger then came out of his cabin, something the Meerkat had never seen before in London. He slowly walked to the back of the bus and gently took the Owl's arm and helped her onto the pavement.

'Remember, don't waste a day!' the Owl shouted over her shoulder to the Meerkat. The Meerkat brushed the soft tears from her face and calmly lay back in her seat, and with no care or conception of time, she dropped into a light, sleep and dreamt of her sister.

Remember don't waste a day

The Meerkat waited in his kitchen with her head in her hands, listening to the raised voices coming from the lounge.

'IT'S NOT WHAT YOU THINK?' the Cat loudly hissed. 'WHAT THE HELL IS THAT SUPPOSED TO MEAN?'

'Look, I need to deal with this situation,' the Bear growled in hushed tones.

'Deal with it, NOW and QUICK' the caterwauling Cat sounded out of control. The door then slammed so hard it shook the whole house. The Bear brushed back the hair from his face as he walked into the kitchen.

'M, how long have you known?' he asked in a whisper.

'I'm sorry, I'm so sorry, I was going to tell you the night you came back after seeing the Jackal, but you were so mad, so angry. I couldn't find the words to tell you, I'm sorry, I never meant for this to happen,' the Meerkat said.

He lumbered around the room in confusion – lost in deep thought.

She waited, too scared to breathe for fear of breaking his concentration.

'I'm sorry, I can't forgive you for the way you behaved with the Jackal – the poor Chameleon, how much it must have hurt,' he said.

She looked back at him in confusion.

'Doesn't she know?' The Bear asked in amazement.

'NO, NO she must never know' she said, flushing with shame. 'I never told her. He was so hurt when the engagement ended – by then it had ended with the Jackal. I was such a fool. She never needs to know', she stammered.

'Look, I'm sorry, I'm going to go, please don't worry about me,' she said, lifting herself off the chair, pushing her bulging weight up with her right hand.

'DON'T WORRY, DON'T WORRY!' he exploded and then he saw the panic in her eyes and dropped his voice to a whisper. 'M you're carrying my baby, how can I not worry?' he said, exasperated.

'I'm so sorry', she sobbed, 'when we got back together, I was so happy. So happy for the first time in such a long time I didn't want to tell you. I didn't want to lose you', she sobbed into her hands.

'I was happy too,' he said, 'did you ever stop to consider that?' He paused and looked into her eyes. 'People told me not to, "she's too much, she's hurt you before, she's too damaged, she's..." but I didn't listen because I loved you. Do you know how scary that is, to love someone that much? To put all your faith and your heart in one person?', he said, 'the risk that takes?' he paused. He put his head into his hands and waited until he could be calm. 'Then I gave you a second chance and what did you do, you abused my love again. Tell me, why should I give you a third chance to hurt me? WHY, TELL ME WHY?' he shouted.

'Because I can't live without you', she said quietly.

Later, he told her he melted at that moment. He knew in his heart that she meant it – her swollen eyes, her jagged, bitten nails, her limp hair, her hollow cheeks, her painfully skinny legs and arms and her small, bulging stomach.

'I'm not sure I can live in a world without you in it, so what do we do?' he sighed.

She was not sure at which point the Bull had joined the Devour board; he just casually strode in one afternoon and took a seat at the head of the table. It had certainly not been agreed between her and the Crab, and the Meerkat's face was red with anger when the Bull confidently walked in the door.

'My main issue', the Meerkat was saying as the Bull interrupted the room, 'is we have a personal responsibility to make sure we protect the sensitive personal data we collect from our customers; they come to us in total privacy and trust. If a third party were to gain access, it would compromise our values', she explained.

Part of the membership of Devour restaurants meant that they had to collect a user's name, gender, location, birthday, education, relationship status and more. As the company was rapidly growing, they had just reached over five million on their CRM system.

'I've heard that some people and businesses don't understand how their personal information is used and I worry that it might be shared in ways they don't want. I'd like us to clear this up now.' The Meerkat finished her statement.

Everybody on the board groaned; it seemed to be the Meerkat's main point of concern, yet the bit that they always wanted to brush over.

'NO, M, I'd like to cover our last six month's progress report, not this, you need to just worry about the next Devour recipe book: you're months behind on this,' the Crab jumped in.

'I'm not sure this is as important as looking towards the future of the company and its security,' the Meerkat frustratedly replied.

'Well I'm afraid I DON'T AGREE, can we have a show of hands on this issue?' the Crab snapped. Five hands raised into the air except one.

'Here, here', said the Bull, thumping his hand on the board room table.

The Meerkat shot him a look of such disgust that he visibly blanched. *How dare he talk*? she thought. She was in constant amazement at his behaviour.

'M, I've found this email trail on the photocopier', her PA handed her the paper, frowning, when she later emerged from the board room, fuming.

From: The Bull

Subject: Membership DEVOUR

Date: April 14, 1998 18:02

To: The Jackal

Mr Jackal,

Always a pleasure.

I've got the Devour membership/customer list, 5M plus names. How much do you want for it? what's it worth to you at EVE?

The Bull

Chairman, Devour Enterprises holdings, inc

From: The Jackal

Subject: Membership DEVOUR

Date: April 14, 1998 18:20

To: The Bull

Mr Bull,

Interesting. How did you manage to get it?

The Jackal

CEO, EVE Enterprises holdings, inc

From: The Bull

Subject: Membership DEVOUR

Date: April 14 1998 19:00

To: The Jackal

Dear Jackal

They trust me, the Dumb fuckers. Want it? How much is it worth under the present circumstances?

The Bull

Chairman, Devour Enterprises holdings, inc

From: The Jackal

Subject: Membership DEVOUR

Date: April 14 1998 19:30

To: The Bull

Mr Bull,

It could make you very rich. Send it over and let's crack a deal,

The Jackal

CEO, Eve Enterprises holdings, inc

The Meerkat was furious. She strode into EVE, *how dare they, how dare he!* The Bull was talking about selling all their confidential data to the Jackal, of all people. The exotic, trendy club was filled with people who turned to look at her. The Jackal had his back to her. His arm was stroking the hair of a raven-haired black creature who looked no older than seventeen. For a moment, his eyes flashed with surprise when he saw her and then he composed himself and smiled. His eyes then glanced down at her stomach and the dark clouds of anger she had seen so many times before appeared, he was livid.

'How dare you come striding into my club with that thing in your stomach, how dare you!' he snarled and his handsome face cracked with ugliness.

'We need to talk, alone', the Meerkat said, looking at the seventeen-year-old.

'GET' said the Jackal to the girl, shooing her away. 'This, I need to hear,' he said. With a swing of her hair and a pout of her swollen, collagen lips, the seventeen-year-old strode off into the crowd.

'I want to talk about our current situation', the Meerkat explained, curtly. She looked for a reaction.

'Current situation?', the Jackal asked. He smiled. 'The current situation of your unwanted pregnancy', he stated. The Meerkat's face twisted in annoyance.

'NO, OUR DEVOUR client data you've bought from the Bull!' she said.

'A small compensation for you getting yourself pregnant. MY MY, you are a crocodile in a petting zoo', he snapped. 'You didn't think I'd let that go did you?' His eyes reflecting a deep emerald green, looked at the bulge in her stomach intensely. 'My wife has got it into her tiny brain that it's mine', he said in disgust, waving in her direction. 'The Bear doesn't want it either, you know', he smugly smiled.

A doubt entered her stomach. Did the Bear not want it? The Jackal laughed at her concerned face, suddenly less confident.

'Fuck you', she silently whispered, but just loud enough so he could hear over the restaurant noise.

He suddenly jumped up and leaned over the small table, shaking his head.

'Tut-tut' he growled, looking at her with a menacing, hungry gaze.

The Meerkat's legs under the table started to shake, she felt sick. The email kept flashing in her mind, wrapped up in images of them together. Questions hummed in her brain. *What was he doing to their business*? *What did he know about the Bear*? *Did he know more than her*? She clenched her 26-week old baby bulge and started to genuinely worry for all of their futures.

'HE DOESN'T WANT IT' he shouted with a hard face, as if to answer one of her unasked questions. Tears sprang into her eyes.

'I hate you' she snarled.

The Jackal recoiled. He then moved around the table so quickly she had no time to turn, his hands slapped her hard across the face and grabbed her by the neck and dragged her close to his face as he whispered in her ear.

'You will never be happy without me, NEVER, ADMIT IT'. He shouted, 'Get rid of that thing and let's stop this charade, then we can be together again like you want – I know that is what you want.'

All eyes in the restaurant turned towards them in surprise. The Jackal paused, looked around at the crowd and at the Meerkat's neck in his hand. He removed his hand from her neck, he smiled gently and stroked her hair like an affectionate lover.

'Now, now my dear, how angry you can still make me', he snarled.

Her body shaking, she rushed to the toilet to be violently sick.

13

'Woman's inhumanity to woman'

Phyllis Chesler

As they drove down to Hastings the very next day, she looked at the Bear. Feeling scared and helpless, the Meerkat tried to put the conversation with the Jackal at the back of her mind, but she couldn't stop her legs shaking. She'd never dare tell the Bear she had been to see him. It had been impulsive, unrehearsed and it had backfired – a red scarf covered her bruised neck. As much as she tried to put it out of her mind, the thoughts kept bursting up, wanting to breathe. What a fool she had been. The Jackal – the creature that she'd known for years – had changed before her eyes, becoming a raw, amplified version of his strange, true nature. His human side finally faded as his true, creative side took over in his pursuit of retaliation.

The Bear looked happy. He was humming to himself and enjoying the breeze flowing through the open window onto his face. She wasn't sure if they were back together again, she was too scared to ask.

'You ok M?' he said, pawing her hand.

'All ok' she said, scared to talk more. Her eyes filled with tears and she brushed them aside. He slept next to her that night and held her hand for most of the night. How much she loved the feel of that hand and the soft purring of his sleeping.

The following morning, they woke up and walked down the hill into the beautiful old town. Everything looked tranquil.

The Meerkat loved the seaside, the energy and power of the sea. She loved the smell of the salt in the air and the way it brushed over her face. She was trying to be calm. The anger and bitterness of the attack and the consequence of the emails had paralysed her. The Bear had become sullen as she refused to tell him what was wrong, he could feel her tight-knit tension, and for the first time, he didn't know quite what to say to make her laugh.

'I know it's tough with work, but please forget about it this weekend', the Bear squeezed her hand.

'I'll try' she said, finding a smile for him.

Suddenly, she grasped at her stomach: tight, radiating, pulsing cramps gripped at her side. The Bear turned in a panic and grabbed her arm as she folded over in pain. Water. Water. Water cames rushing down her legs, warm and intense. A thought filled her mind. *The baby is only 26 weeks old. He's got 14 weeks left to go, what does this mean?* Water. Water everywhere? She wanted to go home and sleep. Sleep forever. As she lay on the pavement, she suddenly knew what this meant. She couldn't keep the baby inside her.

A flashing ambulance arrived, and they shot an injection into her arm that calmed down the pain and sent her to sleep. She must keep the baby inside her, they told her. She filled the time when she woke up writing her work handover notes and emailing them into the board.

The Bear was amazed.

'Is this a crazy work ethic', he asked her, 'or is this because you fear the consequence of not doing them?'

She stayed silent. She knew and he knew.

48 hours later, the labour pain began.

Everyone at the hospital was in silent panic, the baby needed to come out. A nurse held her hand when she cramped and offered no promises or smiles. The Bear paced the room. The Meerkat screamed in pain.

A flashing ambulance arrive

'CAN'T SOMEONE HELP?' the Bear growled at the nurse. Seeing the nurse's face blush, he rushed over to apologise, 'I'm sorry, I'm sorry, but there must be something we can do?'

As the Meerkat screamed again, the room was suddenly filled with nurses and doctors that raced her down into theatre.

spray

'Can you feel this?'

'Yes.'

spray

'Can you feel this?'

'Yes.'

spray

'Can you feel this?'

'No.'

Dive.

Cut.

Pull.

The baby made no sound.

The nurses didn't know where to place the Meerkat in the hospital after the baby was born, with the new mums and their crying babies. Eventually, she was placed in a labour ward, spending hours listening and watching in envy the fat, bulbous, pregnant women brought into the department panting and moaning. The Baby Bear was alive – just. Every morning, she woke up and suddenly remembered their pain.

'We've only bagged him six times last night', the Irish nurse told her in the softest, most caring voice she could manage. Sometimes she wasn't sure she wanted the truth.

Note the definition of bagging: The artificial ventilation performed with a respirator bag, such as an Ambu bag or the reservoir bag on an anaesthesia machine. The bag is squeezed to deliver air to the patient's lungs through a mask, an endotracheal tube, or another breathing device. When the heart stops first in young babies it's used to resuscitate the baby.

They find a small pipette and the Bear, with his big, clumsy paws, had to try and grab the droplets of colostrum from her nipples.

'It's precious stuff, that', the nurse eagerly told the Bear. In deep concentration, he rolled his eyes at the Meerkat.

'Hold still M', his hands shook as he tried to grab at the drops. His concentration couldn't help but make her giggle.

One week in was dark, surreal, filled with guilt and hatred for herself. The baby at first looked misshapen, red and unnaturally tiny. His head was so minute, she could wrap her fingers around it through the incubator window.

'He's doing well, he's a fighter', the nurse told her. She smiled in relief.

Then the next morning, when they walked in, something new was wrong. He'd contracted meningitis and he was back on the ventilator, being pumped full of antibiotics. *What does this mean for him when he's older?* they asked. Nobody knew.

He wore a little cotton hat with a soft, pink ribbon. Yet, compared to his body his head looked huge, his tiny body was shrivelled and skinny. He reminded her of one of those skinned, ducks you saw hanging in the window of the restaurants in Soho's Chinatown – bright red, bare skin and with unrecognisable features. She lay her crying face against the incubator window daily – how she hated herself.

They sent her home alone. The Baby was left in the plastic incubator, struggling to breathe. Devour calls her back, its hunger couldn't do without her. Her weeks were then filled, racing to the hospital at 6am for an hour, then onto the underground into London, then home for 6, back to the hospital.

'Jesus, are you breast pumping for triplets?' she was asked one day by a laughing nurse.

The Meerkat was pumping milk from her engorged breasts every two hours (twenty-four hours a day), then taking it into the hospital in batches to tube-feed into the Baby Bear. The freezers in Devour were filled, shelf after shelf, with bottles of pre-dated breast milk.

'What the hell is that doing in our freezer? For Fuck's sake, M'. The Crab looked at the labels on the bottles, not amused. The Meerkat looked sheepishly on.

Six weeks in, the baby was moved out of intensive care and into a 'Growing room'. He was starting to look more like a baby; he drank her breast milk out of a little cup, like a tiny leprechaun enjoying a beer. They started to see a light appear.

Twelve weeks in, the Baby Bear finally came home. Her four-pound, tiny baby. Back home people, stared at the Baby Bear in restaurants. Not because he was tiny, or his head was slightly too large for his body, but because, even though he mirrored a new born baby physically, he looked at them intently with bright blue, intelligent eyes that followed their every move.

'He's actually 12 weeks old', the Meerkat constantly told their surprised faces.

The Meerkat took another 12 weeks off work and then rushed back. Devour was starving. The conflict. The guilt of each situation, stretching and pulling her in two – how close was she to breaking? she asked herself. The baby was still only sleeping for two-hour stretches before it needed a 40-minute breastfeed, so after a day at work, she returned home to work through the night. Exhaustion. Breastfeeding, working, pumping milk in the day for the night, not stopping, it was relentless! Tired and exhausted, she went home every night feeling guilty for leaving work, but even more guilty for not spending enough time with the Baby Bear. Quick baths, a brief story, a cuddle on his bed, trying to show him she loved him.

A guilty working mum. The Meerkat realised 'love' in its ultimate form when she first saw the Baby Bear. Unconditional and undiluted. She was instantly filled with fear that she would not be able to protect him. The tiny Baby Bear, with thick black hair snuggled into his blanket, his blue eyes like small slits in a carefully cut roll of pastry, not quite round or formed, but a single slit threatening to open.

His tiny mouth was perfectly shaped to make gentle cooing

sounds that called out to her heart and mind, pulling her in. The Bear looked down at his little son and smiled, he too was in love.

The Meerkat once read that an orangutan never leaves its baby's side until it's two years old. They love to nurture, grow, feed, and swaddle their young. Yet, in her endeavours to have it all (or do it all). She learnt the true meaning of the word GUILT. It ate away at her from when the baby was born and she had to return to Devour. A sense of self-deprivation gnawed at her if she didn't manage both brilliantly. But deep down in her soul, it was eating her alive. The loss experienced when the Baby Bear wasn't at her side was overwhelming, so she blanked it out. She didn't race home from work because she had to, she did it because the pull was so strong it was like an addiction. She wished she could find ways where she could carry him round on her back like the baby orangutan.

She Imagined a world where young mums like her could carry their young babies around in this way, on the underground, in the office, during conference calls and working meetings. There would be a chaotic but happy mixture of madness and method. The word GUILT may never have been invented, and her soul would be clean. The guilt was running wild, causing considerable dysfunction and disruption. Her response to the guilt was to work harder and harder and try to contribute more and yet she was wearing herself thin.

In her panic, the emails from the Bull and the Jackal, alas, were forgotten. Much to her later regret.

The Dalai Lama, when asked what surprised him most about humanity answered, 'man, because he sacrifices his health to make money. Then he sacrifices money to recuperate his health. And then he is so anxious about the future that he does not live in the present or the future: he lives as if he is never going to die, and then he dies having never really lived.'

Her mother had a simple understanding of life, and her opinions were strangely accurate. She would often be cited as saying,

'I wish M had taken a career working on the checkout at Tesco, it would make her life much less hassle. Simpler and less stressful.' Or, 'M, you need to be less capable'.

'But Mum', the Meerkat explained, 'I've just opened a big new restaurant'. She sighed, 'Aren't you proud?'

All her mum did was shake her head, questioning the Meerkat's weight loss and her tired eyes.

'There will be nothing left of you if you carry on doing these big business deals that you seem to be finding more important than your own well-being. Your generation will burn themselves out in their 30s', she would say with exasperation in her voice. 'You just don't know how to pace life. You want it all but, in the end, you will end up with nothing'.

The Meerkat had always wanted it all. Her mother knew her well.

Timeline: Summer

The Baby Bear gradually taught the Bear the sincerest form of love – a selfless, overpowering, joy-wrenching love that comes without barriers or personal constraints. The Bear felt its energy and magnetism. He wanted to give more than he had the power or time to offer.

Timeline: Winter

'WHAT? SAY THAT AGAIN', he shouted into the phone. 'YOU ARE KIDDING ME. THERE ARE WHAT? LOADS OF PEOPLE OUTSIDE PETITIONING AGAINST THE STONEWALL EVENT?' his voice thundered.

It was the Meerkat's first night out since the Baby Bear had been born. She'd been invited by two of her gay, flamboyant customers to the Stonewall's yearly gathering at the V&A museum in London. It was a prestigious event and an invite on many levels she just couldn't refuse. On route, while sitting in a black London taxi, one of her customers had received a frantic, heated phone call from one of the event organisers.

'WHAT DID YOU SAY? A HUNDRED ANTI-GAY ACTIVISTS AND LOADS OF TRANS? WHAT ARE THEY PROTESTING ABOUT? OH YES, I REMEMBER. THANKS', he threw down his mobile in disgust, it bounced on the seat and fell to the floor. They both ignored him picking it up and checking for a cracked screen.

'SO ANNOYING!', he exclaimed. 'You will never guess what, darling? He laboured the word *never*. She shook her head in ignorance.

'The anti-gay groups aside, we are always getting that crowd protesting! But now a load of transsexuals are protesting that we won't let them join the Stonewall community, CAN YOU BELIEVE IT?' he shouted. 'JESUS. What's next?!' He rolled his eyes in disbelief and comic shock.

The Meerkat frowned. 'Sorry, I don't understand; the transsexuals aren't allowed to join Stonewall?' she asked.

'NO WAY' he looked at her in disbelief. 'Jesus NO, it's so not right being a transsexual person' he added, shaking his head. 'Not right' both her gay clients nodded in agreement, as she stayed silent in her growing amazement.

They arrived ten minutes later at the bottom of the red carpet. It extended up the stairs and into the V&A. Electric candles illuminated the stairs while red banners floated in the wind with the Stonewall star logo, bold and proud, embroidered onto them. Just to the right of the V&A courtyard, the police had created a penned off area, just like the one used to contain cattle. *The irony of it*, the Meerkat thought when she saw the close proximity of the anti-gay protestors and transsexual protestors, all packed in tightly together. White-haired, middle class, 55/65-year old anti-gay protestors standing next to the flamboyant, expressive transsexuals, with their elaborate beards, colourful wigs and incredibly high heeled shoes. All packed tightly together, yet worlds apart. All protesting in solidarity about the unfairness of the event and community, but both for very different reasons. The Meerkat watched one of the old antigay protesters blanch when one of the transsexuals brushed her arm – a disgusted look crossed her face.

The Meerkat's customers immediately jumped out of the taxis. They had spotted a crowd of friends that they knew and had hastily moved in their direction, glancing back in disdain at the growing protesters. All of the protesters were crammed together into the pen, apart from one.

The ONE stood on the red carpet, handing out leaflets to the incoming crowds of gays and lesbians attending the event. The Meerkat squinted her eyes to see who it was, all alone, there was something about her she recognised.

It was the Chameleon.

Campaigning against the frustration and unfairness of the event, the Chameleon stood alone. She was handing out bright blue and yellow leaflets. She looked triumphant, proud and bold. She was dressed in uncomfortably high shoes, a tight, black skirt and a shimmering, blue top. Her dark brown eyes were covered in shades of bright, blue make-up.

She looks happy was the Meerkat's first thought. She was shining with this new-found purpose in life. The Meerkat's second thought was much darker. She had not told her opinionated gay customers about the Chameleon, and it definitely didn't feel like the right time to do so now. So, she had two choices:

1: To ignore the Chameleon.

2: To walk boldly over and have an awkward, embarrassing chat and risk detection.

Before she had made her decision, the Chameleon spotted her. She started madly waving in her direction. A beaming grin was on her face. The Meerkat wanted to be swallowed up. Instead, a third choice had risen. She surprised herself by walking straight over, holding her hand in the air like an NYC traffic cop stopping incoming traffic.

'I've no time to talk', the Meerkat told the Chameleon in a firm, efficient voice.

The Chameleon looked shocked as the Meerkat rushed by. When the Meerkat glanced back, the Chameleon's head was down, she was looking lost and forlorn.

'Fuck, fuck, fuck', the Meerkat muttered to herself. She tried hard not to care as she walked up the grand staircase and into the elaborate party to celebrate equality.

She tried to forget, mingling in with the world of the flamboyant crowds and museum sculptures, unsure at times which ones were real. The stars of the gay world were out in abundance. All were out to impress, standing proud and ready to show their true colours to the world. Lost and hurt by the slighting of the Chameleon, she swept up glass after glass of champagne, falling and rolling around in the crowds, knocking into people and upsetting their drinks and their mood.

'Oh, here you are, where have you been?' her customer asked in disgust. 'Darling, you've had far too much to drink, it must be the stress of the baby, go home my dear, you are making a fool of yourself and me by association'. Her customer waved her away with a sweep of his hand. She was dismissed.

Unable to sensibly answer, she nodded her head. Bumping and tumbling into people as she left. The air was suddenly hot. She was beginning to feel suffocated by the atmosphere. She didn't belong in this world. She needed to go home to the comforting arms of the Bear and to the soft coos of the Baby Bear. The Jackal leaned against a statue, watching her intently.

'JESUS, how long have you been watching me?' she asked. She could feel his eyes wondering if he should try and catch her. 'Fuck', she whispered, could things get any worse?

'I'm always watching you my dear' he said, and walked away smiling.

She rushed to the exit, looking in fearful anticipation of seeing the Jackal or Chameleon again. How could she avoid them? Only one-way in and one way out. Her drunken brain struggled to function. A crash and a commotion. The Chameleon was standing beside a lamp post, confident and proud in her flamboyant tight outfit. The Meerkat hid in the shadows. She was hiding from everyone, no pride, pure embarrassment all round. A gang of drunken males suddenly appeared from no-where and walked past the Chameleon and paused.

'FUCKING FAIRY' they shouted and started throwing rubbish in the Chameleon's direction, beer cans and coke cans, anything they could grab from the nearby bin – they hit her hard in the stomach.

'WHAT ARE YOU? YOU ONE OF THOSE FAKE WOMEN?' they spat in her face and snatched the wig extension off her head and threw it to the floor, stamping on it with their boots.

The Chameleon stumbled and fell to the ground, protecting her face from the rubbish and insults. They stood and threw cans at her head as she lay in a ball, crunched up on the floor. She managed to rise to her feet and started running. Her shoe was lost and her one high heel clipped away into the darkness. The gang followed, screaming.

'KILL THE FAIRY'

The Meerkat stayed hidden and didn't go to her aid. Shame, fear, bitterness – all gone. How she got home, she never knew. A kind taxi driver, a bus? She was lost in shock and despair. The next day, she woke up with a lingering hangover and a dry mouth. The memory of the Chameleon rose like a growing dread in her mind. The Bear had taken the baby into the spare room, his anger filled their room. She reached for her phone.

'CAM' she shouted into the phone, 'are you ok?' 'Oh my God I'm so sorry, are you ok?' she stuttered.

'M, I'm ok', what do you mean? the Chameleon asked in a calm feminine voice.

'I saw you being abused last night.' the Meerkat sobbed into the phone.

'Oh, that.' The Chameleon sighed. 'I'm sorry you had to see that, it's a common occurrence in my life these days', she said.

'I'm so sorry.' the Meerkat whispered into the phone. 'I never came to help you.'

The Bear was looking at her, puzzled.

'M, this is my life, they don't see me as a 'real woman', they think we are tricksters, sick men who deserve to be beaten.' The Chameleon paused. 'This has happened often to me since I made the change. We are not accepted in most parts of society. We get blamed for everything, from perpetuating gender to our own murders. Forget about potential nuclear war, global warming and the many other threats we face: sometimes you would be forgiven for thinking that us trans people are public enemy number one.' She forced a laugh.

In that madness, they found a new balance without pain. She didn't see the Chameleon again for a long time after that – life just slips by.

Life just slips by.

14

'For a long time, it had seemed to me that life was about to begin – real life. But there was always some obstacle in the way. Something to be got through first, some unfinished business, time still to be served, a debt to be paid. Then life would begin. At last, it dawned on me that these obstacles were my life.'

Fr. Alfred D Souza

Timeline: Summer

They never marry.

The Bear's lack of proposal feels like a daily rejection: a soft, silent resentment gnawed in the Meerkat's mind. They slipped into a comfortable everyday pattern of work, sleep, work, sleep. Time rolled by and they almost stopped noticing each other.

Then one day, their world stopped. The week she found out felt significant, because she was turning thirty. The Meerkat was attempting to win a big contract to keep the hungry beast, Devour satisfied. Their monthly income to keep the company simply turning over had grown out of control. Chasing money was a constant game. One day in that important week, after a shower and a cycle, she stretched her arm above her head as she leaned over her 'PA's desk, rolling it around in a circular movement.

'I think I've pulled a muscle under my arm,' she kept rolling her arm round and round in a cartwheel movement, trying to loosen it up.

'You know M, you've talked about this for the last six months,' her PA pointed out.

'Really?' she asked, with questioning eyes.

'I REALLY think you should get this checked out, I'll get you booked in tomorrow morning,' her PA said.

'No time, no time, the bloody pitch is in two days,' the Meerkat sighed.

'Well, after the pitch. You need to do this. I'll book you in later in the week', her PA said.

By the day of the appointment, the Meerkat had forgotten entirely. She woke up and saw it registered in her daily diary.

Tuesday: visit the consultant 9am.

'Appointment, what appointment M?' The Bear was working from home that day and was surprised.

'Nothing, really', she'd said. 'Nothing at all, just about this arm', she waved her arm in the air.

'Want me to come?' he kindly offered.

'No need', she stated, brushing him off.

'I'll come', he said. *Very odd*, she thought when he insisted.

When they arrived at the appointment, she moved mindlessly through her scans and examination, silently processing her endless to-do list. The Bear watched her intently.

To do:

1: Devour tender next week due in.

2: New business contracts.

3: End of year accounts.

4: New iconic menus.

5: The bloody Devour book complete (the Crab was nagging her on this)

6: Swimming lessons for the Baby Bear, a present from her mother...

At one point, she stopped writing the list. She noticed the consultant's tone had changed, he started talking with unusual seriousness. He caught her attention with the word 'lump, it needs to come out as quickly as possible' his face crumpled in concern. In response to the word lump, the Meerkat started writing notes on a small piece of paper she'd found in her work bag. It could have been an old shopping list receipt or a random paper, she wasn't sure. She was so used to writing notes in her pad and drawing doodles in her books – it kept her on safe ground.

A nurse wearing a formal blue uniform and a soft, sympathetic smile walked in through the door to join the consultant. The piece of paper slipped to the floor. The Meerkat bent down to pick it up. She watched as her hand shook. As they started to explain what they'd found, she wrote notes faster and faster, trying to capture every single word she was being told. They layed out formally the treatment options for her survival: mastectomy, chemo, radio. When she asks them where it is, they don't know exactly, apart from somewhere under her arm and in her breasts.

'We need to wait and be patient', her consultant explained.

'WAIT AND BE PATIENT. WAIT AND BE PATIENT' she screamed the words in her head.

The most urgent and most immediate thing she needed to know was, WHERE IS IT, had it spread? Would it kill her? She daren't look behind her because another face, which would look even more scared than hers, was sitting right behind her. The Bear stayed silent.

In an instant all her deadlines d i s a p p e a

All her priorities were recalculated. She'd found out that when listening to lousy news, her hearing ability stopped functioning. She'd made this discovery earlier in life in a noisy intensive care neonatal unit, when the Baby Bear arrived fourteen weeks early. It was an odd contradiction to her true nature. She was so used to listening intensely, recording conversations with pinpoint accuracy, but when bad news was told to her, she could not hear, record or remember a thing.

Everyone stopped talking and looked at her. The Bear took her hand and led her to the car. They both sat in shocked silence on the way home. Their life had stopped in its tracks. She watched with envy through their car window as other people continued on with their lives, carefree. The radio blasted out the theme to the Lion King, 'The Circle of Life' filled the car with its irony. 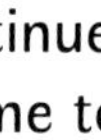

The news brought home one great truth about her life: the ease with which the big crises can wipe out the small ones that seemed so critical just a moment before. All the anxieties and pitch preoccupations evaporated with the sudden recognition of what really mattered. She was again reminded of the impermanence of life. One question rolled around and around in her mind. The cancer: did she bring it on herself? She'd always just wanted to be successful, to work hard, but TIME now stood in the way. Being successful in the world around her was being defined by:

Who worked the longest hours.

Who went the longest without a break.

Who slept the least.

Who responded to an email at 11:30pm at night, or 5am in the morning.

A time famine. Then she passed this self-destructive relationship with time on to her child. Rushing him to swimming, then to shopping, then to the nursery. In her race for life, had she taken on too much stress over the years? Poor diet, eating on the run, lack of exercise. She was a modern woman, and she'd been told she could have it all. Yes, it all!

'Bloody hell, I've been doing it all in one big go for years, and it's finally burnt me out.' She tried to explain her feelings to the Bear that night.

'A kid, setting up a new business, running a house, keeping customers happy, being an amazing mum that's at the nursery gates as often as I can, at sports days, trying to help at the school, being a *50 Shades of Grey* sex goddess in the bedroom–' She looked at the Bear's handsome face as she ranted. God, he was getting better looking as he got older. Every day she looked in the mirror she was looking older, her mouth had started to sag, and small lines were forming under her eyes.

She was gradually melting.

07884567889...

The Meerkat saw the number flash up on her phone. She'd not heard from him in a very long time. She paused. They had managed to stay out of his way, politely declining invitations and always checking first who was going to any event or party. The uncomfortable moments avoided at all cost.

'M, I've heard the news', the Jackal said. He was breathing heavily down the phone. 'I'm worried, I need to see you'.

'There is nothing to say', she stated.

'I'm so scared, I can't sleep' he said and started to sob into the phone. 'My wife's friend died last year of the same thing, she was gone six months after the diagnosis. Jesus M, I can't imagine the world without you in it, what are you going to do? I NEED to see you!'

The Meerkat felt her throat constricting and a wave of panic gripped her body. He was voicing her biggest fears. Ones that she had tried not to think about. She'd had a wave of concerned friends texting, crying, calling, sending her flowers and she was touched by their gifts – but were they all actually thinking she was going to die? Had they already written her off?

'I'm sorry', she said into the phone and cut off the call.

'Who was that?' The Bear asked when she placed the phone down onto the table. His concerned eyes scanned her face.

'No-one, No-one important', she said. 'Just somebody else thinking I'm going to die' she said. She fell to the floor, sobbing, 'and I probably am'. As she cried into the soft rug, she suddenly felt a body lie next to her. Two big arms wrapped round her.

'I don't want to ever hear you say that again,' the Bear sobbed into her hair. 'We are going to get through this', he said. 'We are going to get through this.'

'How do you know, how does anyone know?' she sighed.

'You're like a cockroach M, you could survive an apocalypse!' Her sobbing turned into a half-laugh and half-cry, and as they lay in each other's arms on the floor of their lounge she wondered what she would do without him.

She was glad it was her.

Her nutritionist friend aptly put the birth of the premature baby (26 weeks) and the cancer down to the fact that she needed two bodies to maintain the pace she had set herself in life and that two warnings were surely enough. A spare body in the wardrobe suddenly seemed like an enviable thing to have in her closet.

The spare body theory: She wished she could open the wardrobe, and there was one other version of herself, but this one was perfect.

Two healthy breasts

A full, lush mane of hair

Limbs that weren't swollen and sore

Bright, shiny green, happy eyes and no stamped in, mind-altering memory of the cancer growing inside her.

She read endless books on how to help herself through the process: vegan diets, green juices, low protein, no red meat, no alcohol, no sugar, no dairy, no stress. The last one, STRESS was hardest to avoid. The business was not doing well. The pull of work was hard to ignore. She needed to be at Devour not worrying about cancer. The first six weeks after the news, she headed into work every day and pretended it was not happening. It was her way of dealing with things: ignore things, and they will go away.

'M, when are you going to face this?' the Bear's eyes pleaded with her.

'You need to take time out for the operation, the cancer needs to come out, it's growing', he softly explained. Her blank 'front' looked back at him. She was in flat denial, numbed to pain.

The problem was the Crab had left her in a paralysed shock.

As the Meerkat reached out her to for love, sympathy and understanding, she hit a solid, cold, brick wall. Fear, anger, resentment? She couldn't tell. The thick shell was wrapped so tightly around the Crab, there was no way to know. Was she fearful for Devour? Her life ending? The Crab's own mortality? Every time she met her in one of the Devour restaurants, the Crab would turn her head and march quickly away. The Crab didn't want to see, so she put her head in the sand. The Meerkat waited for her approval. Her consultant rang her daily, pushing for a date for the operation.

The Cancer GREW

'25% survival rate over the next five years' she overheard the oncologist say one day when she was being briefed about her impending chemo treatment. She panicked and froze.

'75% chance of dying?', she asked quietly back.

'Jesus M, WE NEED TO SORT THIS OUT.' The Bear's soft approach had stopped weeks before, and now he was screaming and shouting in her face.

As she looked into his eyes, she saw he was scared. Not just scared, but petrified. The light peppering of grey on his head had turned in a matter of weeks into a snow storm, and his eyes were etched with dark, black shadows.

'What will they find?' she asked the Bear robotically, 'How big is it, where else will they find it?' He held her hand and sighed.

The pleading in his eyes finally broke her heart, and her 'front' dropped to the floor.

The Meerkat was busy shopping at John Lewis, the big new store in Kingston. She was looking for a new double bed for their spare room, they'd had a sofa bed in there for ages, and she was sick and tired of rolling it in and out. My goodness, rows and rows of beds. Different headboards and quilt covers. So many to choose from. One with a smooth, grey, fabric headboard featuring a beautiful, deep-buttoned headrest caught her eye. She ran her hands over the softness of the material and impulsively jumped onto its plump, white, crisp duvet, lying snugly inside its embrace, purring with happiness. *I can't sleep here* she thought, but suddenly she was too tired to care. Comfort and darkness enveloped her as she fell asleep.

She woke up what felt like moments later in a raw panic. 'JESUS why is it so hot in here?' she was burning up. Oh my God, under her arms is on fire, the pain is raw, intense and acute.

'M, M, M!' she could hear someone shouting her name from afar. She tried to turn around to see who it was but her head was so heavy, the pain so intense.

'What, what, what?' she whispered back. Her throat was all dry and her voice crackled in pain.

'M, M, M' they shouted, and she could feel them shaking her, but she couldn't see who it was.

Her arms were not just burning, *oh my God I've been shot,* her brain scrambled to comprehend. The pain was just unbearable. WHO'S SHOT ME? she screamed into her mind. She was flailing around on the bed, the soft pillows and quilt were now quite literally suffocating her, she couldn't breathe. Then she remembered exactly where she was. The realisation hit her hard, as everything came flooding back. A smell of antiseptic filled her nose.

Doctors running frantically around her, nurses whispering loudly, machines beeping.

'She's waking up, thank God, her breathing is back to normal', she heard them frantically whispering.

'Let's try and make her comfortable – she must be in lots of pain'. A fair-haired nurse squeezed her hand and looked into her eyes and smiled. 'Love, love are you ok?' she asked.

The Bear had squeezed onto her single hospital bed before she'd gone down to surgery. Holding her hand until they had come to collect her, so cold, so scared. She'd felt like leaping off the bed and running away, she could barely control the panic and the urge to bolt. Aware of her violent shivering, she was wheeled down to the theatre. As she was injected with the anaesthetic, everything started to go black, and her last thought was, *I wonder if this is what it's like to die?* Just blackness and nothing more: it filled her with sadness.

Two days later when she could finally think clearly again and the cloud of morphine had lifted, she opened her eyes and she found the Bear asleep in the chair beside her.

'Sshh', the nurse said, holding her finger over her lips.

She could see in his hand, he was clutching a small, gold bracelet with an ornate clasp. The nurse followed the direction of her eyes resting on the bracelet.

'In the eight hours that you were in surgery, he couldn't bear the wait, so he went out and came back with that', she explained.

'He's not slept in days, let him sleep now,' she explained. 'I can't bear to see him cry again'.

'Living in fear is just another way of dying before your time.'

Mike Cooley

In ten years' time, the Meerkat doubted chemotherapy would exist. It would be seen as barbaric. She'd read that in the early 1900s, in their attempts to rid women of cancer lumps, they would chop out vast areas of a woman's arms and chest. But sometimes they chopped so much away, that their shoulders simply collapsed, flopping onto their chest. But for now, chemo was her only option if she wanted a statistical survival rate of higher than 25%. She had no idea what the journey ahead looked like.

'Being diagnosed with cancer is like being bombed, and you have to crawl out and get on with your life the best way that you can,' the psychiatrist Dr Drake told her one afternoon when she was struggling with her mind. The doctor stood at her bed and gave her a business card. 'Come and see me', she said.

'I'm OK, don't worry about me', the Meerkat sighed.

'No, I am, you need to speak to someone: you've been through so much – they can treat your body' she said, waving at the hospital ward, 'but we also need to treat your mind', she said, tapping at her head.

Many hands were trying to help her after the bombing, but she felt stuck in a deep, dark hole she couldn't crawl out.

She dug out the card days later. She felt lost.

'I'm so incredibly lost', she'd told Dr Drake. 'I just can't work out exactly why and how to put it right. It's like a thick fog I can't see through, it's like having a head full of bees,' she sighed.

'Head full of bees?' Dr Drake said. 'Why?'

'It sounds crazy,' the Meerkat explained, 'I've seen the effects of death at an early age. I deserved to die, not her. It was like somehow I'd cheated death, and this was now my time.' Dr Drake pushed the tissues towards the Meerkat, and she wiped the tears from her eyes.

'You mentioned "her" a lot in there, who's "her"?' Dr Drake asked gently.

'My sister', the Meerkat said. It was strange to hear the words on her mouth again after so long.

They sat there for a moment and let the words sink in. Dr Drake let her sob until she was ready to speak.

'I don't want to talk about what happened to her', the Meerkat said, 'I can't do that, not now!'

Dr Drake was very calm.

'Be kind to yourself, you've been through so much, there must be a silver lining in this.'

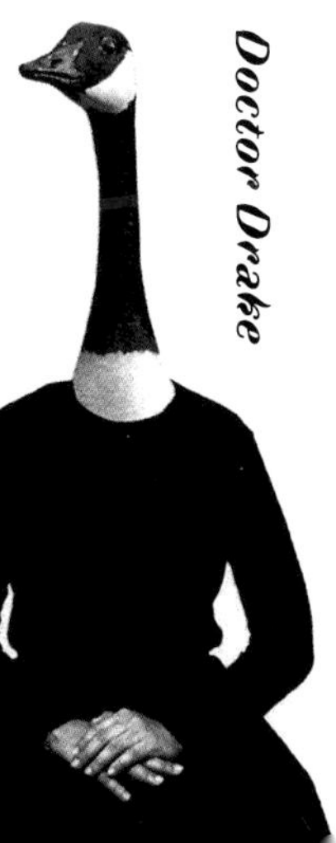

Doctor Drake

The Meerkat almost laughed. 'What do I do?' she said desperately. 'How do I fix this? I'm so scared of death!"

When the Meerkat was younger, she felt that death was a long way away. She almost believed that their time on the earth would last forever and they would all have endless streams of hours and adventures ahead. Then she realised one dreadful day that she'd been kidding herself for a very long time. First her sister and now her. The moment they were conceived they were programmed to die; for her, death could be any day now.

'Be kind to yourself', Dr Drake repeated as she smiled at the Meerkat, her whole face crinkled with affection. The Meerkat's head dropped.

'Every-day, say to yourself, I'm going to live to be ninety,' Dr Drake suggested. 'None of us knows when our time is up. But living in fear every day isn't living. Fear is like death' she said.

The Meerkat chanted day in and day out.

The Bear became her rock. She only felt safe when he was around her. Her fear was crippling.

'Hello', the Crab said smiling as the Meerkat opened her front door.

The Crab had never been on the Meerkat's door-step before.

The Crab's hands were laden down with two large shopping bags and two bottles of wine.

The Meerkat's hands were laden down with six drainage bottles filled with toxic fluid.

They looked at each other intently.

In their past, there would have been numerous bottles shared between them. Both toxic and dangerous in their own way.

'Here', the Crab jabbed one of her bottles at the Meerkat. The Meerkat looked at her hands full of bottles and back at the Crab and frowned. The Crab pulled back the bottle, pouting.

As the Crab got tangled up in with the shopping bags, the bottles of wine and removing her sunglasses, the Meerkat got tangled up in the six tubes coming out from holes in her breast and her back. They were draining off the dangerous fluid from the cavity that once was her breasts. *Such irony*, the Meerkat thought, as the Crab composed herself. But the Meerkat's bottles were far from being filled with wine, and the Crab was far from being a friend anymore.

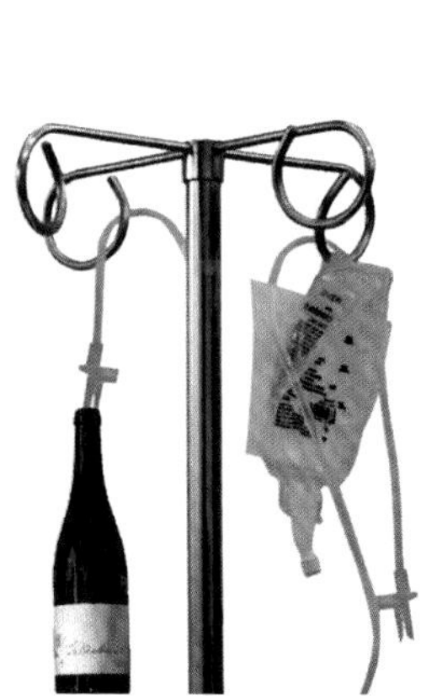

The Meerkat waved her in, it was cold outside and the wind swept in down through her hall.

'Chilli?' the Crab asked the Meerkat, shaking the two heavy shopping bags as she walked into her kitchen.

The Crab took out the chilli ingredients and layed them neatly out on the kitchen work-surface. The Crab, an expert cook, threw the ingredients into a large pan with ease. Before long the smell of the chilli made the Meerkat's mouth water. She'd not eaten properly for weeks, and she was suddenly very hungry for life again. The Crab somehow always had that effect on her.

'Are we OK?' the Meerkat dared to ask, knowing that they have not been OK for a very long time.

'We will always be friends', the Crab snapped. 'Way after all our other friends, husbands and lovers have gone, we will always be friends', she softened and smiled. 'I'm sure of that'. The Meerkat had not seen that smile for a very long time.

'Let's eat, it must be ready now', the Crab gestured to the chilli. Two old friends enjoying dinner, having happier conversations of times gone past. Nights out, softball games in the park, holidays in Ibiza.

'Remember that time M, when we were on the tube, and you got your ponytail caught in the door? When you could eventually pull it out two stops later, it was covered in dust and all black.'

They both laughed hard at the memory. The Crab suddenly jumped, a text had bleeped loud in her phone. She snatched it quickly from the table, but the Meerkat had seen.

Text: You were only going to be 15mins, WHERE THE HELL ARE YOU? Don't FUCK-ing forget. The Bull.

The Crab's face crumpled and blushed. They both looked at each other, passing knowing looks with thousands of unspoken words.

'Oh, before I forget' the Crab blustered, I've brought something I need you to sign', The Crab dug out a large envelope casually from her bag and handed it to the Meerkat, in it was a thick bunch of papers. 'Just sign there', she pointed at a page at the back. 'Nothing important', she muttered.

The Meerkat looked back at her with questioning eyes and signed. The Crab left shortly after.

To be 'in control' before the chemo started, which in itself was a joke, the Meerkat cut her hair short and wore a cold cap to try and keep it from falling out. She had an optimistic hope that she was going be one of the lucky ones and keep all her hair. But after chemo, she realised that it was not going to happen, when her hair fell through her hands like snow in the shower. The first chemo made her so sick she struggled to breathe through the retching. The second made her ache, the third made her feel like she was rotting inside and out and the rest she couldn't remember because it became a blur.

On a good day, she could cycle to the nearby park and feel invigorated that she had the energy and power to move around again so freely. Her body, so taken for granted previously, she now worshipped.

On a perfect day, she'd feel so lucky that she was alive and that she'd have more time with her baby. In the rat race of life, this was the first breath she'd taken in years, and she didn't know how long it would last.

On a bad day the chemo was as near to dea as she could get.

She couldn't sleep. She'd struggled to get out of bed except to be sick, her hair fell out, her eyes itched, her toenails went black,

to be 90. I'm going to live to be 90. I'm going to live to be 90. I'm going to live to be 90. I'm going to live to be 90. I'm going to live to be 90. I'm going to live to be 90. I'm going to live to be 90. I'm going to live to be 90.

The treatment ended, and instead of feeling relief, she felt scared. So scared. Now the treatment had stopped, would the cancer grow again while it was not being watched? The question whirled around and around in her mind. Passion and drive gone. She'd worked hard, driven for success, friends valued her. Happiness, who had got the time to measure that? Life was racing by, and there was so little time for reflection.

Then stop.

She'd got the diagnosis. She didn't see it coming. She had no control over it. How bad was the cancer? It was her only question, and no one around her could answer her except 'JESUS'.

She knew she needed to act quickly, maximise her time, but do what?

Set up a charity, run a marathon, give up her job, climb a mountain, go to India, move to a new house, spend more time with her friends, spend endless hours baking with the Baby Bear. She had no idea, but the feeling would not go away. She'd not seen death for many years in real life, but now its presence surrounded her.

'The Meerkat dream has stopped', she told Dr Drake on her next visit.

'But now I have a death dream. I keep dreaming about a room filled with ancient, old creatures dancing to the hum of life. They are so old that you don't see them around you. They have been handed over to the care of the hundreds of nursing homes, they hide from us our mortality and our impending terminal prognosis. They have lost their value in society, so they have been tucked away, someone else's problems. They smell of death, the nappies of the old wrapped as tightly as if they were new babies. We don't want to see them.'

'Why not?' Dr Drake asked.

'So we can convince ourselves death doesn't exist', she explained. 'So, death is never seen on our doorstep, it's too close to home, we are not allowed to talk about it ever', she said.

'The fear of death can help us live', Dr Drake explained. 'It helps us live more authentically'. She paused. 'When working with cancer patients, I have found that the patients have changed the way they lived after diagnosis. They were less concerned about which parties they had not been invited to', she said. 'Instead, they were more likely to be attuned to the change of seasons. They said no when they didn't want to do something and spent more time with the people that they loved to be around – there is lots of good in this.'

'What's so good?' asked the Meerkat.

'The diamond in the coal is that you have learnt in your 30s what most people don't learn till they're in their 90s, when they are about to die. Be happy about this, you can make changes – life can be short, so live it to the full', Dr Drake explained. 'Don't think you're a ticking time bomb', she smiled. 'Think about what you can do with your time and live life to the full.'

The pressing and straightforward problem was the Meerkat had again experienced mortality. No, not just learnt, but felt the feeling with all her mind, body and soul. She felt that intense feeling of her impending death, so then, how could she go back to her old life?

What could she do with that knowledge? Bag it, hide it, stay busy and ignore it, tuck it away in the far corners of her mind and pretend she'd never experienced it? It was like she'd learnt life's biggest secret and she felt a rising need to share her knowledge: but was it something others would want to know? She tried to forget, but my God it came back to her daily, like a sick feeling in her throat, rising and threatening to vomit up at any moment. She felt silly for giving it so much weight. But once she had understood that TIME was her biggest commodity, not money, clothes or work, the burning question became, how did she use her time wisely and how long did she have?

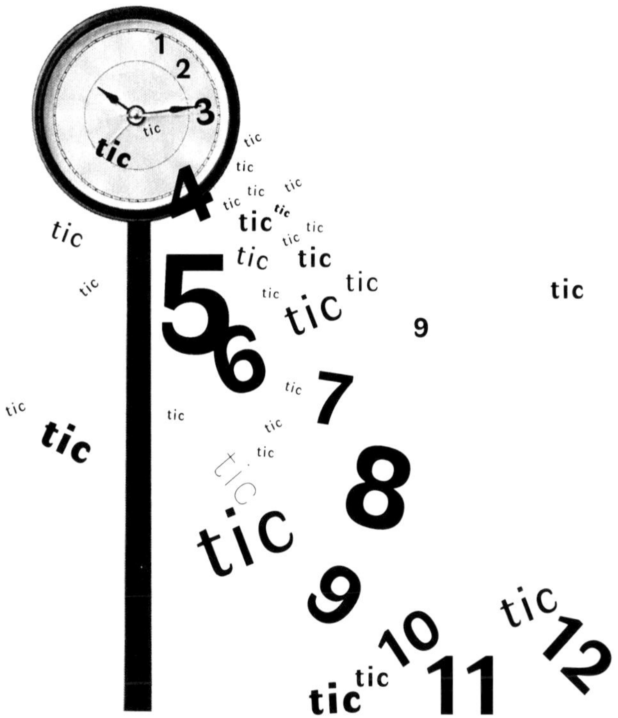

20%

50%,

75%

99%

through her life?

Nobody knew.

Ignore medical statistics, they didn't help, they just scared her half to death. She needed to act quickly, use her gifts, but do what? She had no idea. But the feeling of time would not go away. Her new, misshapen and scarred, flat chest reminded her, not how bad things were, but how lucky she had been.

She was now living her life in three-month intervals, paused at each point in time by an MRI and bone scan. There was a deep dread before each scan happened, in which she convinced herself it had come back, then an enormous sense of relief when each time everything looked clear. Living in this constant fear made her life feel very acute and real, like the feeling of walking up a huge mountain even when you have terrible vertigo: you're half scared to death, but also half in wonderment of the beauty of the world at such a great height. So carefully balanced: with every new insight, sometimes comes enormous fear.

'The Chemo has pushed you into early menopause' the consultant told her casually one day.

'Early menopause?' she questioned. The Bear went very still.

'There will be no more children for you, I'm so sorry.'

She wrapped her arms around the Baby Bear that night when he was asleep and cried into his soft hair.

Timeline: Summer

The Meerkat's cancer had caused her own mother to rot. She couldn't bear any-more pain from her children. Her mum lost weight like her, stressed like her, lost sleep like her, and gradually the Meerkat found her mother turning more and more into a version of her. She told the Meerkat one night, 'I wish it was me'.

After chemo five, her mother tried to help lift her mood by driving the Meerkat round to see the Crab in her big new house in King's Road. The Bull and the Crab were drowning in a luxury of space. The Meerkat wondered if the Crab, seeing her looking so poorly, would crumble and love her again? Two stone lighter, no hair, no smile, all went unspoken. With pride and glee, the Crab instead showed them round her vast house, filled to the brim with her collection of luxury clothes, bags and matching shoes.

New L.Vs

New Michael Kors bag

New cashmere coats

Cooing over every item.

The Meerkat's mother stayed strangely quiet. As they drove home, her mum stated, 'She hasn't changed.' She paused to consider her words. 'She is exactly the same, determined, driven and insanely focused.' She shook her head with bitter disappointment.

when you love a flower

'What is the difference between 'I like you' and 'I love you', beautifully answered by Buddah: 'when you like a flower you just pluck it. But when you love a flower you water it daily. One who understands this, understands life.'

Buddah

Timeline: Winter

The atmosphere was toxic. The Meerkat couldn't keep her mind off her latest test results. It had been twelve long hours since her latest MRI scan, and she'd forced herself to go into Devour. The Bull was there ALL of the time. She tried to concentrate on baking and developing new menus, but the fear of her bad results was so debilitating she struggled to think. *Why hadn't her consultant called,* she thought? Her phone sat quietly on her desk next to her computer, but it didn't ring. She picked it up and checked that the ring was turned on. It was fine. It was on full volume. *But why wasn't he ringing?* She asked herself again.

She then went to the toilet, threw up and splashed cold water on her face. Still no call. She'd been holding in the panic for so long that she was breaking inside. With a resigned sigh, she slid down the toilet door and sat on the floor with her head in her hands. The door of the next toilet door slid open and the Crab marched out of one of the cubicles and viewed her slumped on the floor. The Crab calmly washed her hands in the sink, refreshed her lipstick in the mirror, pouted and left the bathroom, slamming the door.

Not a word was spoken between them.

'M, we need to talk' The Meerkat's PA told her when she returned to Devour.

'Can we go out and grab a coffee?' The Meerkat could sense her panic.

They walked to the nearby Starbucks and ordered coffee.

'Something's up, M, and I'm worried', her PA said. The Meerkat was expecting the PA to ask about her latest results.

'Worried?' the Meerkat asked. She paused.

'I'm sorry, there is no easy way to say this, but I've found out the Bull has sold all the latest DEVOUR customer members' data to the Jackal. I watched him download it onto a hard drive, place it into an envelope and post it to the Jackal at EVE'.

Her PA sat silently, waiting for her response. 'He even knew I was watching and didn't care. He winked as he slipped it into an envelope.'

'JESUS!', the Meerkat shouted at the top of her voice. Everyone in the coffee shop turned around and looked in their direction.

'I can't stay, I'm sorry. I'm resigning. I don't want any part of this, it's rotten', her PA stated.

The Meerkat was stunned into silence.

The Meerkat's phone rang, its ring echoed round the coffee shop. All eyes were on her.

She snatched it off the table with such a force that it slid off and onto the floor. She dropped to her knees and scrabbled around, trying to grab it before the ringing stopped. Just in time, she slid the button across and received the call.

'Hello,' she panted into the phone.

'Hello', a calm voice replied. It was a voice she'd grown to respect so much, but dread in equal measure. Her consultant breathed heavily down the phone.

'There is no easy way to say this, but we've noticed a shadow on your liver, you need to come in straight away and get it looked at. I've scheduled you in for an operation in two days' he explained. 'That's the earliest we can get you in with all these NHS cut-backs' he sighed.

'Oh', she managed to whisper. She stayed on the floor and crouched with her head in her hands. Time stood still as she curled there, shaking.

With no conception of time, she felt two powerful arms around her, the comfort of the hug almost too much to bear. The Bear gently lifted her up and carried her into the car, taking her shaking body home.

Death had arrived at their door.

'Learn to understand your dreams', Doctor Drake had said. 'They are your mind giving your brain messages, you need to listen hard to their meaning'.

THE DREAM THAT NIGHT: The Meerkat was standing with the Crab outside their two-up two-down house in Liverpool. The house had fallen into disrepair. The paint on its windows was cracked and flaking, the black door had a large hole in the bottom panel which had been covered by a piece of MDF and a few nails. The Crab looked at the Meerkat in surprise: there was so much warmth in those eyes. They opened the door and walked hand in hand along the hall. The wall-paper was hanging off, there were large holes in the wall that showed the wall joists behind. They walked into the lounge, and the old leather brown sofa was torn. The curtains were falling apart, dirty and stained. The carpet had been ripped up in parts, and the wooden floor was teeming with insects. Dirt and stains dripped down from the walls behind them, and the ceiling had holes so large you could see the Meerkat's bedroom above and then beyond into the attic.

The Crab touched the walls, stroking them tenderly. With the other hand, she reached out for the Meerkat and held her hand in hers. She smiled, and with the smile, the walls, floors and ceilings started to ripple, and the house was perfect again. The Meerkat was perfect again. Exactly how they had left it, years before. Photos of them everywhere. Smiling together, lying outside the pub on blankets, attending their graduation ceremony, posing for pictures outside crowded pubs, playing softball in the park. Everything was perfect.

The Meerkat woke up the next morning and a letter from Devour had also arrived on their doorstep.

'Silence is sometimes the best answer

Dalai Lama

They met in a lively restaurant on the riverfront. It was filled with smiling and laughing business people in sharp city suits and yummy mummies with cute, cooing babies. The Meerkat's stomach

'Is this the Crab?', Doctor Drake asked. 'Does this describe her relationship with you – is she your friend, is this someone you trust?'

The Meerkat stopped breathing, the shock and the realisation sinking into her mind.

Back to the café on the river, with the soft, cooing babies, the yummy mummies and the posh city boys. The Meerkat digested what the Crab was saying, the trick she had played. The Crab smiled back at her. The Meerkat leaned back in her chair, and that's when her eye caught sight of the Jackal and the Bull sitting at the back of the restaurant, intently watching from afar. The investor. The Jackal was the new majority shareholder. It all made sense in one sudden moment. The Jackal was laughing and smiling at a comment from the Bull, as he glanced over, he gave her a wink, his control back in place.

'It's over', the Meerkat whispered to the Crab. 'We're done.'

The Crab reeled back as if she'd visibly hit her. She flicked to her phone and deleted the Meerkat's number.

'Fine!' she snapped.

15 The letter

'Hello, hello, hello' the voice says. The Meerkat can hear the Bear's soft voice, it touches her ears, but she can't quite open her eyes, they are so tired and heavy. All she wants to know is, did they find any cancer? Her panic is beyond words. She feels his hand and manages to open her eyes.

'I'm so sorry', she said to the Bear.

'Sorry about what? You have made my life worth living', he said.

'Tell me', she stammered.

'I've got good news and bad news.' The Bear sighed, holding a letter in his hand.

'The bad news first', she replied. I'm sorry', he stated again as he handed her a legal looking document, from the Devour board. She opened it and read it with silent contemplation.

She leaned back in her hospital bed and sighed. A shot to her heart. As she lay there, she broke into an enormous smile.

'The good news must be they haven't found any cancer?' she asked the Bear, as he broke into a smile.

'You outran science!' he reached for her hand and rested his head on her chest.

'If there is any religion that could cope with modern scientific needs, it would be Buddhism'

Albert Einstein

Timeline: late Autumn

The Elephant returned to London in the late autumn. November is one of the worst months to visit the capital: it's cold, wet and grey. It's the darkness before the light of Christmas ascends on London. When all the Christmas decorations go up, it turns London overnight into a magical city. It was unexpected, but as always, perfectly timed in life's doorway. The Elephant had visited the Meerkat twice during the chemo, and on each visit, she told her she'd almost expected to arrive and see her broken and dispirited, but instead each time she met a fighter, determined to win.

'Jesus M, you look shit, what the hell's happened? The Elephant asked. Huge, black-grey shadows hung under the Meerkat's eyes.

The Meerkat handed the Elephant the DEVOUR letter. Her face changed from looking calm and serene to anger.

'FUCKING HELL, THIS IS MADNESS!!!' Her Buddhist calmness dropped like a rock to the floor in her amazement 'My God, no wonder you look so broken, I couldn't work it out when you opened the door, I thought the cancer had come back, Christ M.' She was cross. 'Get out M, get out, this is making you ill. NO, this is your illness, and even though it's going to be tough to get out, this is your cure', the Elephant shouted. 'This path is wrong for you.' She paused and sighed. 'Carry on in this life, and you will kill yourself.' The Meerkat had never seen such anger and fierce resolve in her before.

As she related the story about the Crab, the Bull, the Jackal and Devour, the Elephant got more cross.

'The investor's condition was I stay in the business, without that investment, Devour could be ruined, my shares will be useless and all that hard work–' The Meerkat sighed.

'The red ribbons are deeply intertwined between you all, and they won't let you go easily, but you must cut all ties with them,' The Elephant said.

'They are DEVOURING you, can't you see that?'

'But how do I let go, when I'm so tired, just so tired of fighting'? the Meerkat cried.

'Be like a samurai: strong, determined and confident but with honour and integrity!' The Elephant exclaimed. 'Don't be a dog! You must never be a dog in a fight,' she sighed.

16

'Confusion is the beginning of understanding, the first stage of letting go of the Neuronal gossip that used to keep you chained to concrete ideas about who you are and what you are capable of, confusion, in other words, is the first step on the path to real well being.'

Yongey Mingyur Rinpoche

Timeline: Winter

'I'm so angry and confused', the Meerkat told the Bear. Legal letters were flying back and forth; the battle had begun.

'You are in danger of catastrophic thinking, you need to calm down', he replied.

'What's catastrophic thinking?' she asked. She was feeling bleak, dark and hurt.

'Ok, for example, two groups of overweight people take part in a study: they all have for many weeks been participating on an extensive diet', he paused. 'One day they are asked to partake in an experiment. Both groups are given several, huge, chocolate cakes. The first group is told to take a slice. Each slice is only 160 calories. The second group are just told to help themselves with no idea of calories. The first group just takes one slice of the 160 calorie cake and really enjoy the taste of the sugary treat. The second group take a slice, thinks *sod it, this is delightful, my diet is fucked anyway* and then proceed to eat more and more slices, stuffing their bodies with this sugary overload,' he explained.

'My point is', said the Bear, 'If we view any problem we have with a catastrophic mindset, then you will act and behave in a wild, random, uncontrolled manner. But if we gauge ourselves and keep our minds level', he said, 'we will see the world as it should be, with grace and determination'.

She smiled and tried to reason with her own mind.

'If you think you are too small to make a difference, try sleeping with a mosquito.'

Dalai Lama

The Meerkat finally settled out of court. Her shares sold.

TIME.

Time to focus on the Baby Bear, who'd been so quiet and sullen. He sensed when she had become sicker. The more sick she had become, the more he stuck to the Bear – just as nature intended. The young always stick to the healthiest, strongest parent.

Now she had time to make amends.

TIME to make his packed lunches.

TIME to stop feeling overwhelmed.

TIME to stop behind unkind to herself.

TIME to end the guilt.

TIME to breathe.

TIME. That's all we have.

The Meerkat slowly walked along the South Bank and it reminded her of the first conversation she'd had with the Elephant years ago, about life connections and ribbons. It had made so much sense in those dark times. How far she had come since she first met the Chameleon in the steam room. How much change had occurred in both of their lives. The Chameleon had found out about the Meerkat's cancer battle and was desperate to see her. They were set to meet at 1pm in the ground floor café at the Tate Modern. The memory of seeing the Chameleon being beaten by the thugs was still ingrained in her mind, closely followed by her guilt for not helping, Jesus, sometimes she was shit.

She was the first to arrive. She sat quietly drinking a cold glass of lemonade while waiting, watching the creatures running all around her. Groups of happy school children skipped by in twos, reminding her of the Baby Bear, how fast he was growing, how serious and grown-up he looked in his small school uniform. His tiny head would stick out from under the duvet, covered in thick, black hair. Her heart soared every morning when she saw his face peering out. A perfect, mini version of his father, with wide brown eyes and curly, animated hair that wildly stuck up in the morning. So far from the tiny child they had brought home from the hospital.

'Be prepared to take a year off work', the consultant had said. 'He might have eye, hearing, breathing issues, we don't know', she sighed.

But he was perfect, determined and strong – just like his father.

The Chameleon suddenly appeared from nowhere, flashing her big, wide smile as she walked over. She was wearing elaborate makeup, a large, pink dress covered with butterflies and very high pink and gold shoes. Everyone in the room watched her clip across the café. The butterflies fluttered with every *clip. clip. clip*. The Meerkat stood up and embraced the Chameleon.

'When I heard the news, I was so scared for

you M', the Chameleon frowned as she took a seat opposite the Meerkat while ruffling up her dress. Her voice sounded unusually high and more feminine. The Meerkat looked at her in a puzzled way and pointed at her throat.

'Laryngeal surgery, surgery on the voice box to make me sound more female' the Chameleon said, blushing. 'Anyway, less about me, how are you? Here you are looking so well, for someone who's been through so much, if not a little too bald and skinny!' the Chameleon smiled and sympathetically touched the Meerkat's hand. 'Has the cancer gone?' she asked with fear in her eyes.

'I'm not sure', the Meerkat answered and paused. 'Who knows, it's been like an unwanted guest that can come and go as it pleases. To be honest, I'm not sure what hurts most these days, the Crab's betrayal or the cancer, it's so hard to weigh anything up anymore', she said, picking up her bag and pulling out her peach lip gloss.

The Chameleon laughed.

'M, I used to love wearing your peach lip gloss, did you ever notice how quickly it ran out?'. The lip gloss tasted like ash in her mouth. It was strange how it still hurt the Meerkat, these little confessions. The Meerkat frowned.

'How are you, Cam?' the Meerkat asked.

'Well, I, on the other hand, am busy screwing my life up,' Cam said. 'I caught my lover fucking a friend at a party, the cheek of it!' she complained. 'Also, to top it all off, my lady bits are now not working.' The Meerkat looked back at her bewildered. 'The daily routine of flushing out this hand-made vagina you wouldn't believe', she explained, pointing down to her lap.

The Meerkat with no breasts and the Chameleon with no penis: it all suddenly seemed so surreal.

'I need to know what happened, Cam. Don't you owe us both this?', the Meerkat asked.

The Chameleon shifted in her seat, and a sweat broke out on her brow.

'I don't like talking about this, it's in the past, right?' the Chameleon said.

'It's in the past', the Meerkat said softly, 'but, I still need to know. I just keep asking myself why didn't you tell me,' she sighed.

'When I was at boarding school, my parents' expectations were so high, and I was bullied.' The Chameleon paused. 'I was not sporty, in fact in everything physical I was slow. But I was also knowledgeable, like a child prodigy. Every week I would walk from the primary school to the secondary school to take advanced maths, my first A* GSCE in maths I gained at twelve. My parents were over the moon. All the teachers loved me. But this didn't seem to make me popular at all with my peers', she sighed.

'Why?' the Meerkat asked.

'I just don't know, M', The Chameleon answered. 'All I know is, that it peaked when I arrived at secondary school, every-day there would be violence directed towards me. Then I started having this fantasy of being a girl. Maybe I would be safer as a girl?' she paused and wiped the tears from her eyes.

'But a girl, Cam?' The Meekat asked.

'As a girl, I thought, I could be free of this, but still, be academic. Girls can be smart too', she sipped gently on her drink. 'It became a fantasy that grew every day, my dream, but not something that could really happen to me. Then I met you', the Chameleon said and smiled. 'In the beginning, it was lovely, we got on so well. But then it turned dark, and we both grew miserable. Remember the butterfly?' The Chameleon asked.

'Of course, I do' said the Meerkat. 'I never killed it you know, you never let me explain, it was dead before I stepped on it. They only live for two weeks you know, such a short cycle of life'. The Meerkat sighed.

The Chameleon reached down and played with a few of the butterflies on her dress. She stroked their wings and tenderly touched their tiny cotton eyes.

'You know what, for two weeks I would take that carefree life', the Chameleon said. 'I knew you didn't kill it, that wasn't why I was crying', said the Chameleon. 'Don't you know why?' she asked, surprised. 'I was daydreaming in my hammock about being a girl, and then you appeared, so perfect, everything I ever wanted to be'.

When they had finished their lunch, they walked down the South Bank, the Chameleon wrapped tightly in a bright pink, furry coat and heels so high she could hardly keep her balance. The Meerkat, in a short leather jacket with soft white trainers, held her arm to stop her from falling. As they passed by the carousel, its vibrant colours and joyous sounds drew them in. They watched the carousel's wooden animals riding around in circles, never really leaving or arriving. A white fawn, a black raven, a fox, jackals, an elephant, a crab, a chameleon, a bear, a meerkat, a bull, a blue sea horse and a mad otter in a hat.

'I love you M, can you ever love me again?' The Chameleon suddenly asked.

'I've not got my heart to give.' The Meerkat smiled sadly. The Chameleon blinked back her tears.

The Meerkat held out her hand to the sad, timid Chameleon. 'Come on let's have a go?' She smiled like a demure Victorian lady and took the Meerkat's soft hand and sniffed.

'Why not', she laughed, whilst crying. She'd known the answer.

Out of respect for the Chameleon, the Meerkat didn't pick the bear on the carousel, but instead choose a blue sea horse. Its mane was blowing in the wind, its scaly skin rubbed against her thighs as she leapt on. The Chameleon crawled on the chameleon. She gently wrapped her arms like a lover around its neck and stroked its shimmering skin like she was somehow comforting it. Round and round they went, laughing and smiling with the music playing in the background, the cold wind blowing, waking them up and filling them with the feeling of life. Flying wild, flying free, moving up and down, the magic of the carousel. The carousel animals came alive with the movement, blurring between wooden characters and real animals, all brimming with human qualities and expressions. The Bull's huge neck, which folded into his huge muscular shoulders, snorting out smoke through billowing angry nostrils. The large Bear, fierce one minute then cuddly the next, padded around the carousel in huge bounds. The Crab, with a large, red shell and sharp, long claws and small, beady eyes had a little boy on its back, his wary eyes looking out for his mum. The soft, grey circus elephant had a chain around her foot and sad, soft, melancholy eyes. A pack of hunting jackals chased after a meerkat and the one that was the brightest and most alive. All in a chase to nowhere, never able to catch each other up.

Two mad, laughing friends remembering their youth again. The animals they rode had enjoyed these rides for centuries, they were beyond time, and for these brief moments, it took away their perception of time. The music and the movement transported them into a magical place: she wasn't the Meerkat, she wasn't the Chameleon, they were both Mary Poppins: 'Practically perfect in every way'.

Practically perfect in every way

For those moments, they were both blissfully happy and perfect again. They quietly parted later, there were no kisses or hugs, just a polite bob of their heads. The intimacy of touching too raw. As the Meerkat walked away, she watched the Chameleon's shoulders slump and listened to her high heels tap away into the distance – wobbling as she went.

'If everyone in the world stood in a line M, you'd be the last person that can help him', her dad had said years before.

It played out over and over in her mind as she walked away and got the train home to her Bears.

She never saw the Chameleon alive again.

17

Why, she could never be sure. Maybe his near-loss of her made him wise up, or perhaps he'd grown to love her soft, new, vulnerable side. The Meerkat and the Bear had known each other for many years when he asked her to marry him. So much had happened since that first day she met him on the train. They were in a beautiful, natural, organic hotel in Bath and he'd arranged for her to have a two-hour body massage. It was months after the last chemo, and the Meerkat still felt broken. When she had been massaged from head to toe, she almost cried in bliss and tranquillity. If her body could hum with contentment, it would have done. She'd lost 17 pounds, her bones were poking through her skin, and she hadn't got a hair left on her body, except for the long, fake, wig, but she was alive.

The Meerkat walked into the church, arm in arm with her father, to the song 'Wild Horses'. As the crowd appeared in their seats before her, she started to sob, shaking with each step – so many faces that she loved, all in one space, she couldn't quite believe it. The Bear and the Meerkat's friend the Robin had prepared a hand-written speech for the church. Standing on the podium in the small, beautiful old church, crammed packed with friends and family, the Robin stood there waiting. With tears in her eyes, she began her crafted story. The Robin had wild, red, curly hair, an infectious smile, high cheekbones, long slender limbs and sharp, curious intelligence that radiated out from her eyes. Everything she touched, built or created was exquisite. Her writing, her gold, hand-stitched picture for the Meerkat's hen weekend, her cupcake hat, crafted for their wedding party. Everything was so delicately considered and made with a passion and love that could only end in near perfection.

Colourful creatures:

'This is a story about two of the most colourful things on God's earth. Unique and unusual, exceptional and extraordinary. She, a Meerkat with a hint of baby deer, with a gorgeous golden coat and a highly contagious laugh.

He, a big brown Bear with a faint whiff of primate and curiously small paws. One fortuitous day, many years ago, their paths crossed. The Bear immediately noticed the Meerkat's vivacious and charismatic playfulness, her free spirit and her irrefutable tinge of naughtiness. And she clocked his hairy rugged good looks, his rogue-ish ways, quick wit, wildness and his discernible prowess on the air guitar.

They were immediately drawn together by a mutual passion for life and a particular affection for celebratory gatherings, where she would showcase her rare, spontaneous and specialised dance moves and he could indulge his penchant for Robbie Williams and soft rock and perform equally maverick manoeuvres. They also shared a love of, and loyalty to, their fellow animals. She, patient, kind, loyal and supportive, (occasionally dizzy, slightly bonkers). He, honest, hilarious, sincere, intuitive, (often uninhibited, occasionally inappropriate). Both thoughtful, insightful, and caring and dependable and generous in the extreme with their time, their food stores, their highly sensitised ears and their candid wisdom. It is essential when describing these creatures to observe and revere their contradictions, despite the time spent playing freely, they both toil and labour hard. She shows the Meerkat's gifts of drive and focus, tenacity, flair and fearlessness and gifted creativity, admired greatly by the other creatures. He, gregarious, charismatic, modest, brilliant, creative (especially with magic marker pen holders, again, unusual for bears) and dedicated, though occasionally a little late for things.

Together, they created a beautiful burrow (or cave) and they produced one tiny male offspring, showing character, humour, playfulness, sensitivity and the stunning aesthetic of their parents, adored beyond question by both. It has been observed that the Meerkat and the Bear speak their own language, an expressive and nuanced form of communication which other creatures often copy but rarely understand: chibby, chibby, kiddy kiddy, ursha momma, shabba, foible, wilf, shniddle, noodle, mange.

Their life together has taken them across varying terrains, a luscious meadow, at times a jagged rock-face. A vibrant and flourishing forest and an arid desert. Every so often, he lifted her up in his bear embrace and helped her over the turbulent water. In the waterfall, he offered her protection and there were times where she guided him through the undergrowth and showed him a lot of love and affection, always at each other's side when needed but knowing when there was a wish for solitary rejuvenation, for the Meerkat to do a little bit of sentry duty or feline capers, or for the Bear to forage for fermented fruits or slumber a little in his cave. (Or partake in some gummy bear gambling).

On this path, they found that she was brave and determined, capable and delicate, vulnerable and strong and he was inspired by this. They found that he was devoted and reliable and honest and that his humour was the best medicine. Together, they discovered that their laughter broke through the most challenging of challenges. Together, they have already lived a lot

of life, entertained many different species and brought a great deal of colour and kooky nuttiness into their habitat and their fellow creatures love them for this. The world is more fun, with them in it. Fun and sunshine – there's enough for everyone. And there is a lot more life to be lived in the wilds of Wimbledon. Wherever it may take them, I know that life won't break them. Don't stop believing. Hold on to that feeling. They've got each other, and that's a lot'.

The Meerkat's heart soared, as wave after wave of emotion swept over her. Everyone she loved in the world was in one confined space – except for two. She kept expecting to see her best friend burst in at any minute, with her flaming red hair and an elaborate outfit. Surrounded by their amazing friends, all fabulously colourful, they danced, cried and laughed all day. They had introduced a hat theme for the afternoon, and their friends rose to the occasion with elaborate headwear: white Indian headdresses, bird headdresses, every animal you could imagine – including an orange Bear balaclava.

The Meerkat kept catching the Jackal staring at the Elephant with an odd smile on his face. How beautiful the Elephant looked, the Meerkat thought. She had on a beautiful, long, grey silk dress which draped off her shoulders and emphasised her curves. She wasn't surprised by the Jackal's intense gaze. The Meerkat had tried to persuade the Bear not to invite him, but his loyalty to the Jackal, even after everything they had been through, seemed strong. Yet, every time the Meekat looked over at the Elephant, she seemed unsettled. She kept nibbling at her nails and pulling at her long hair in a nervous, twitching movement that the Meerkat had not seen since their final days in Liverpool.

'Are you ok?', the Meerkat asked. The Elephant looked startled.

'Sure, sure', the Elephant said quickly. The Jackal took that moment to confidently stride over. 'Have we met before?', he asked. He reached out his hand and stroked the Elephant's arm – she recoiled. The Jackal smiled. Had the Elephant met him before, she wondered? The Elephant excused herself and rushed to the toilet with intent.

'What do you see in that ageing Bear?' the Jackal had asked. Trying to compare himself to the Bear in some way. She laughed so hard in his face that he sulked away with his tail between his legs.

The Meerkat had only recently heard that his wife, the Raven, had left him for her young, stylish yoga coach. It followed her discovery of a memory stick filled with hundreds of photos of the Jackal having sex with multitudes of different creatures in various exotic positions.

'How could the Raven treat him like that?' he had complained to his friends at the wedding while eyeing up the Elephant. He couldn't keep his eyes off her.

When it came to the speeches, the Meerkat had decided to give her own speech; she felt that she had things that she needed to say, things long kept hidden. She stood up at the table and pulled the white, handwritten note from her pocket. She looked at the Bear first and then took in the smiles of her friends.

The Meerkat's speech

'Having one day in our lives with all the people we love, who have supported us and made our experience really enjoyable is the best thing ever. I can honestly say we have had a life jam-packed with magnificent friends. So, thank you for sharing this day with us. Now, a few thanks of my own,' she smiled. 'But – cue some favouritism – over the years. I've really realised how truly great my group of friends are. They have taken magnificence to new heights. Never in my whole life have I felt so supported, loved and cared for. In short, you are brilliant! All beers are on me for the next year.' She smiled at the Elephant's frowning face.

'I also have to say an enormous thank you to my incredible mother and father, for literally everything. I've never felt anything less than lucky to have been born to such an extraordinary couple. My folks aren't just my parents, they are my best friends, my biggest supporters and an all-round selfless pair.' She smiled at her parents, sitting next to her at the table and paused.

'There are two creatures that I so wish were here today. The shame of it is, one didn't come through pride' – she paused, she was sure everyone knew who she meant. 'Well, the other, that is my sister.'

'Today, I want to remember not only my sister, but the people who tried to help her the day she was killed. I just wish with all my heart she could be here today. She was the most thoughtful, kind, loving and fun sister there ever was. I want to thank the residents and the delivery man who called 999 and who simply stopped and were there for her when she was knocked off her bike. It brings me some peace to know that she was not alone at that time.' Tears sprang from her eyes, the memory was so crisp, as clear as the day she was told.

Back to the days in Liverpool, a week into living in the tiny house with Ele

The Meerkat was living in Liverpool for the summer, in the strange little terraced house with the Elephant. She knew, as soon as she opened the door to her parents, she knew. Something was wrong. Why were they there? She'd only been gone a week, her brain flustered confusion.

Then she looked into her mother and father's eyes and she knew. She felt their profound, longing, devastation. The acuteness of their depth of misery. She tried to push the door shut, she didn't want to know.

'GO AWAY' she shouted in a panic *'GO AWAY'*. The Elephant

appeared behind her and pulled open the door and laid her hand on her shoulder.

The Meerkat's mother's body shook with sobs and she fell to her knees. As her dad picked her up, he sobbed.

'She was knocked off her bike by a car, and the driver didn't even stop', her dad said, shaking. 'He simply drove away and left her to die, alone at the side of the road – alone except' Her dad then started to cry – 'alone except for a neighbour and delivery man, they held her hand when she died. When the ambulance came, it was too late, too late', he repeated.

The Meerkat never went back to her home again. That home, that life had died with her sister.

She refused to go to the funeral.

She refused to believe she had died.

She refused to live in a world without her sister in it.

So, she pretended that she was alive and would talk to her every-day in the mirror.

The wedding speech cont...

The Meerkat drifted back into the NOW, that's what she had been told she needed to do by Dr Drake. Doctor Drake and the cancer had changed so many things. She had to acknowledge she had lost a sister. She couldn't stand at her wedding and pretend her sister didn't exist anymore. She owed her that much, and the police had called only yesterday and said they had an anonymous tip they were investigating on who had killed her.

She glanced at her softly sobbing parents and felt the small, wooden girl figure that the dressmaker had sewed into her dress – her sister was there with them; she could feel her presence in the air. She let a sob slip from her mouth and a single tear roll down her face. Then she held her head high and continued.

'Lastly, I want to acknowledge all those who have lost a loved one due to a crime, and for whom their case is still unsolved, my heart goes out to you'. The tears rolled down her eyes and onto her dress. She forced herself up straight.

'And finally, thanks to my pride and joy: my Bear, or, adeptly nicknamed (by himself) my ROCK. From the first time on the train I saw you, I loved you, but how lost I got. I'm so sorry for that.'

She looked down at the Bear's handsome face and grey peppered hair, a face that years ago she had fallen in love with from the minute he had ambled onto the train. But, how lost she had got along the way, the path she had chosen at times was so destructive and self-harming. How she wished she could turn back time and avoid all the hurt.

'In our lifetime together, there have been so many fun adventures, and even in our sad times, the Bear could make me stop and laugh. So, thanks to the Bear for being my best friend and lover. Without you there, making me laugh at the most inappropriate moments, my life would have been a much duller place. I never know

The shock of seeing the news when she was casually flicking down her Facebook page nearly stopped her heart.

She frantically began searching the Chameleon's page, and as the news unfolded, she lost her ability to breathe. Bewildered friends and lovers posted their dismay.

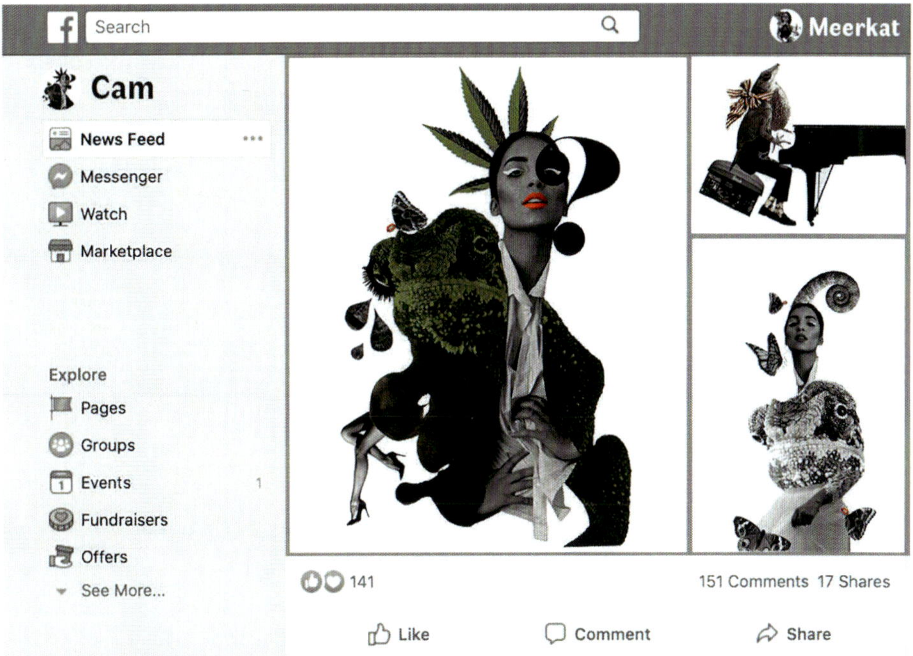

View previous comments

Rest in lovely peace lady'

CAM

The hormones make me feel so up and down. One minute I feel moody and the next minute really happy... I hate the dark moods

Like Comment Share

View previous comments

Rest in lovely peace lady'

CAM
Life is to dark, where is the light in this life. Help. I need some light.

View previous comments

LOL Cam, hope you're ok? BM xx

CAM
Just read the Telegraph (UK) Sex change regrets: Gender reversal surgery is on the rise, so why aren't we talking about it? Why aren't we talking about it? Not sure I agree, not sure anymore, I've worked so hard to become a woman...

View previous comments

Hold on in there, Jay x

Reply

No regrets Jay, but not benefitted much psychologically, been tough xx

Reply

Tough one, don't overthink on it, Jim x

Reply

Really Cam. We love it – think Bruce Jenner, Carol x

Reply

Every person has the right to be treated equally and with dignity and respect regardless of gender! Stu x

Reply

Trans lives are not a debate. F**k this guy and f**k this article. Sue x

CAM

:-)

View previous comments

RIP

Reply

I can't believe it merely devastated, Scotty xx

Reply

RIP Cam, love you always, Jo xx

Reply

WTF Cam!!! Tim xx

Reply

We will always love you xx Carol + MJ

Reply

RIP mate, so sorry KL x

Reply

Jesus Cam - Anon x

Reply

Please don't let it be true, I love you so much Bx

Sent by the Chameleon's mother... with a hand-written BITCH scored across the letter with thick, black pen...

To my lovely M,

I can't find my place in life. Inside, as you know, I have the heart of a simple and soft woman, but I am a woman who was born with a physical deformity. I have lived most of my life pretending to be a man to avoid destroying loved ones close to me, but as I did this, I only destroyed myself.

For the most part of my life, I have lived being mentally paralysed, too stubborn to give up on life. Of course, there has been some good stuff, but it felt like I was always looking through fog at life and a world that I didn't have full membership of. It was hard to appreciate that I had anything to do with any of the good stuff happening around me or any right to believe I could deserve any of it.

When I transitioned into a woman, the feeling of being right and belonging was immense and complete, and to my surprise it was instant. That doesn't mean a problem free, soft and fluffy life, it just meant I had the privilege of facing life living as the real me. This is a luxury that most take for granted. When I chat with people, some say I must be proud, and I must have incredible courage. Neither of which is true. Of course, I thank them for their kind words, but I don't have courage. I am certainly not proud of being Transgender, people do not have to be proud of their gender, it is just who they are.

BITCH*

Nothing lately seems to go right for me, every time I find happiness it slips out of my grasp. The latest one is too hurtful to write about. I just want you to know that I love you, even though I recently heard you never loved me, I still love you. I know about your affair when we were still together. I wish I didn't but I do.

The only thing that I have left of our time together now is the beautiful, red hammock. I found it wrapped in my wardrobe last night and the pain of the discovery, the knowledge that I will never feel happiness or joy like this again has become so acute that I just wonder if I can carry on. Burying my face in its fabric I can see you walk down the path and I can almost smell your scent, the lavender perfume you so loved to wear. I imagined the red and green butterflies again, fluttering around us. My heart is sad M, but then I saw a light – a hope of a better life, another life.

So, my love, I now want to be brave and take a rest from this world I can no longer bear to be in. Take care and remember me, I hope we can meet in another life and be happy again, till then.

Yours forever, your soul mate.

Cam xx

* Written by the Chameleon's mother

The Meerkat agreed with his mum for the first 10 seconds, then had difficulty shaking it off.

Police Report Template

POLICE REPORT

Case No: 345627654

Date: 00.00.00

Reporting Officer: XX

Prepared By: XX

Incident: REPORTED SUICIDE – WAITING FOR WITNESS TO COME FORWARD

Evidence ROPE

A 35-year old transexual woman was found hanging by a hessian rope, taken from dismantling an old red hammock in his unbolted bedroom. The cable was found attached to two suspension points (one end connected to the window panel and the other side to the door knob), and the middle part of it used for the binding of the neck. She was separated from her fiancée many years back and had been staying in a co-operative house with friends. A suicide note was found at the crime scene.

An unknown male was seen leaving her apartment earlier on in the day. If anyone can identify this person, please come forward as we'd like to eliminate him from our ongoing investigation.

'The essence of ordinary life is suffering, one of the most effective antidotes is laughter – particularly laughter at oneself. Every aspect of an experience assumes a certain type of brightness when you learn to laugh at yourself.'

The Joy of Living, Yongey Mingyur Rinpoche

The Meerkat spent days in a state of shock. Her memories became more precise and more surreal. She would see the Chameleon's face in all of her dreams, she could smell the scent of her clothes and feel the butterflies flutter around in her mind.

'Only time can heal your pain', Doctor Drake told her when she visited her. 'Time's a healer.'

For the first time in years, the Meerkat wished for time to speed up. The loss she felt was mixed with remorse, guilt and a sense of hopelessness. Could she have helped her? Something didn't feel right about it all. The question dominated the Meerkat's mind day and night, rolling around, never fading. It was crippling and she felt a primeval need to flee. She felt suffocated by her surroundings.

Only weeks before, she had starting to feel like a baby deer, whose legs had stopped shaking in fear and whose limbs had become stronger. Her unwanted guest had not returned and she had started to feel alive. She'd starting to walk with more confidence. To run with increased speed and intent and taste the wind and emotions of the world around her. It wasn't without fear. Scans every six months scared her to death. During these, she would shrink down into the tall grass and hide from life again. The fear felt like death. Deep down, she knew that she would have to leave the comfort of the tall grass as all baby deers eventually feel compelled to do. She had started to move forwards towards what mattered and find purpose again. Her inner energy and curious nature took over her instinct to hide. But now this, she was back to hiding in the grass again. The Crab had cut her out of her life, the Chameleon was now dead, and the Jackal had disappeared. Out of the five who had shaped her life so acutely, two of them were now gone. She was left with an overwhelming feeling that no one had won. The experience left her hollow and looking for answers.

While the Elephant had no solid proof of the power of the Buddhist faith, she had told the Meerkat about the goodness of their beliefs and their healing qualities. Left devastated by the Chameleon's death, the Meerkat dipped her toe into the Elephant's world and booked her flights to India. The Elephant's gift to her was to take her to the monastic college, the Shabling Institute of Buddhist Studies, for a week in Dharamsala to listen to the Buddhist teaching of the honourable Tia Situ Ruma.

Could she find a light again and lose the pebble that had built up in her throat, threatening to choke her?

'Happiness is not something ready-made, it comes from your own actions'

Dalai Lama

As they walked off the plane into the Indian sunshine, the heat hit them, covering them with an immediate blanket of sweat. The nine-hour flight had seen them squeezed into an old rickety plane, that bowed and rattled and creaked with the wind. They landed bewildered, exhausted and half scared out of their wits. Death seemed always on her doorstep.

'Come on, let's get a taxi into the city', the Elephant said. She was animated. She was back home.

'I love India', the Elephant said as if feeling the need to explain her excellent mood after the fearsome flight. England was no longer her home. Her heart belonged in India and every day she spent away from it felt like a wasted day in her life.

The taxi that took them from the airport was a battered, white Citroen. Each panel of the car showed a scar from a previous collision. The friendly taxi driver was keen to hear about London. He seemed to have a longing for, as he called it, 'the fast life in London'. He gleamed with anticipation as she described the city and her life within it.

'So, what's it like in the Natural History Museum?' he asked. His 100th question since they got in the taxi.

'Well, it's certainly not as hectic as here', the Meerkat laughed as they drove out of the airport into the hum of the traffic.

'The Natural History Museum is an amazing place', the Meerkat said, 'Stuffed animals, bones of animals – existing or extinct. It's fascinating, free but also a bit sad to see all those stuffed animals with dead faces'.

'Free', the taxi driver said in amazement. The stuffed, dead faces bit passed him by.

The Meerkat soon realised why there were so many bumps on his car as they squeezed into five lanes of traffic in a motorway with four lanes. No one seemed to pay attention to the white lines on the road. There were just thousands of cars all squeezing in the same direction. Bumper to bumper. Each inches away from each other. Beeping and honking so they could press along the insanely busy lanes.

'This is manic, but everyone is so polite, why?' The Meerkat asked.

'Oh my', the taxi driver said, 'there are huge consequences if a driver causes an accident and they are foolish' he answered, shaking his head from side to side.

'I once witnessed a load of drivers and their passengers turn into a frenzied mob in seconds', he said shaking his head again vigorously. 'They surrounded the accident and pulled the careless driver from the car and beat him mercilessly. There is no tolerance for bad driving', he said with a sigh, 'but these are the unspoken rules that keep the road in some sort of order', he said.

Life was so delicately balanced. Millions of people all squeezed together in such a hot, melting place of experience. Such a fine line between life and death. Through the car window, there was such a mix of smells and sounds that overwhelmed her senses: plastic burning, urine, spicy food, overbearing perfumes, smoke from fires on street corners as they burnt plastic containers. Noise from traffic. Screaming children. Banging from buildings being constructed everywhere she looked. Most of the buildings looked like they were part of a scene from an apocalyptic movie, filled with holes, crumbling and battered, while others looked like gleaming concrete and metal western constructions.

Delhi was a city of contradictions. Deep poverty contrasted with enormous wealth. Skinny, starving people contrasted with the bloated tummies of the wealthy, overfed Indians. There were gated, rich corporate companies' headquarters with vast fountains, filled to the brim with water, mini waterfalls and jets. Yet in front of the gates, small children were waiting at a single water tap. Waiting to be offered up to an hour's worth of water when the city's water pipe was turned on. A day's quota needed to be collected between 5-6pm. They could see the children race to the taps, loaded down with containers of every size, shape and colour to obtain this precious commodity.

The Elephant navigated the city like an experienced traveller. She navigated the begging people that seemed to surround them wherever they went by handing out small change that she'd stored in a large purse in anticipation of the pursuit. She never turned away a hand. She had a kind, beautiful face that children and women gravitated to. They were surrounded on many occasions with children with half limbs, no feet or hands, but the saddest of all was the begging children carrying tiny babies, holding them out, pleading for them to help. The Elephant had a solid resolve. Even the most extreme poverty she seemed accustomed to. Her pennies flowed, and her eyes were always dry. The Meerkat couldn't understand her attitude at first.

On their second day, the Meerkat watched the same small children running around naked, standing in tiny bowls being washed down at the roadside by their mums. They were living in shelters made from sheets of cardboard and corrugated metal. Her heart was wrenched by the thinness of their tiny bodies and the dirt on their faces. Yet, the more she looked below the surface, the more she could see a massive sense of community. These weren't children that were not loved or cared for. They just had so little that the splashes of water, the tickling of their mums, the laughter surrounding their play, made their small faces light up and she could see that they were happy. Life experienced in the now of the everyday. Happiness didn't mean fancy clothes and an abundance of plastic toys and iPads. It appeared that they had so very little, but actually, they had so much. Within a matter of days, the Meerkat went from being scared of this enormous, smelly and dusty city to loving its sense of community and culture. Its apparent lack of money, and yet its obvious wealth of happiness bubbled hidden away beneath the surface.

'It's a place that has claimed my heart', the Elephant said on the third day. 'It's filled with people living life to the full. They are surrounded by so little, but yet they feel so content, I envy them,' she sighed.

24 hours earlier. --
--

'Jesus M', this is crazy, the Otter whispered to the Meerkat. It had started to rain and icy droplets were glistening on his fur and running into his large, brown eyes. The Otter must have wished he hadn't put on such a thick concealer, as it was running into his eyes, making them sting. The Meerkat laughed. A propensity for not liking water was outside of his true nature.

'Maybe that outfit doesn't help' she said, pointing at his tight-fitting leather dress and his high Louis Vuitton shoes.

'When you said we were going to see the handsome Jackal,' The Otter whispered, 'I never imagined for one minute it would be to scamper through his garden and stare in through his windows.' The Otter tried to rub the earth marks off his dress, but quickly gave up after his frantic brushing movements made no difference.

She'd woken at 3am, wondering about the police report. The need to know more about the Jackal was gnawing at the Meerkat's soul. He had disappeared since the wedding. Who was that man leaving the Chameleon's house? She suspected she knew. She could see images of the Chameleon hanging from the red hammock, the memories created a panic in her. A sense of urgency. It was all her fault. She had bought the Jackal into all of their lives.

'Quick, the light has come on in the lounge. Let's duck behind the pool changing rooms', the Meerkat said, as she skilfully rolled behind the pool house and waited for the Otter in his incredibly high shoes to follow her. His clip, clip, clip echoed around the pool.

'Christ, these LVs are ruined', he panted when he got close.

'Jesus, take them

off and hold them in your hand', she whispered.

'Bare feet?' he gasped, 'Never.' His face looked disgusted at her suggestion. She smiled at her beautiful friend, so innocent and yet so provocative in the world.

The Jackal's house wasn't an average two-up two-down Victorian. It was, instead, an exclusive gated mansion in the suburbs of Surrey. He was a neighbour to the Chameleon's parents. His house, with its pool, extensive outhouses and gardens, looked like it was from the middle of the 18th century. It was in fact only built a few years before, under the controlling eye of the Jackal. As she leaned against the edge of the cold stone wall, the Meerkat could see the roof of the summer house over the Jackal's fence. She remembered afternoon tea with the Chameleon's parents in that house. She cringed. That was a lifetime ago. The anger rose in her throat.

'The basement lights have come on, let's go and take a look,' the Meerkat said, her anger spurring her on.

'What the hell are we looking for?' the Otter said. 'He's hardly going to have photos of the Chameleon displayed in his basement cinema room'.

The Meerkat could tell he was secretly enjoying himself. His sedated life of smoking dens and transvestite clubs was a world away from this middle-class suburban world. The Meerkat crawled to the basement window and lay flat against the cold, wet flag-stones.

'You owe me a dress and new shoes', the Otter said as he slid in beside her.

Both of their eyes grew wide as they looked into the basement room. It was luxury personified. Rows of velvet green cinema seats fitted with popcorn and drinks holders lined the room, . There was a large mirror covering the whole of the ceiling, making the room seem like an endless atrium. The Jackal sat in one of the large green chairs, naked. The Otter giggled. 'An amazing species', he whispered. The Meerkat nudged him hard. The Jackal got up and walked in their direction and flipped on an old cinema film projector. His naked body created a shadow against the wall. The Meerkat could see the Jackal's alter-ego shape silhouetted. A long nose, sharp, pointed teeth and intense eyes.

'Wow M, what a lucky girl you were' the Otter giggled, his perfect, white teeth shone mischievously, not looking at the silhouette but directly at one element of the Jackal's human form.

'Sssh', the Meerkat said with a grimace.

The enormous projector screen flickered. The Meerkat could see a small Jackal cub on the screen, running around screaming and laughing and a large Bear scoop him up and cuddle him. A tiny Bear appeared in the corner of the film, cautious and timid. The tiny Bear looked at the Jackal and the mother Bear and ran to hide behind his father. His father, a magnificent Bear, lifted him up onto his shoulders and ran with him around the garden till he laughed. The Bear and the Jackal's childhood, the Meerkat thought, had the Bear ever seen this footage she wondered? The Jackal started madly laughing. The reel ended and a new film started. The Chameleon appeared dressed in his favourite butterfly dress, a pink wig and bright red lipstick. She was playing the piano in the Jackal's nightclub, Eve. The Chameleon hammered the keys and the music swung into a hypnotic beat, the Jackal appeared in the corner of the screen, smiling. The Chameleon focused all of his attention on the end of the Jackal's nose.

The Meerkat and the Otter didn't breathe.

'Fuck, that's Cam, what the hell was she doing at Eve?' the

Meerkat whispered angrily. The Otter looked sheepishly back.

The Jackal started howling with laughter like a trapped animal.

'M, we need to get out of here,' the Otter said, suddenly worried. His animalistic senses could pick up an odd feeling in the air. A smell of madness.

Suddenly, the Jackal stood up and walked to the front of the room and fiddled with one of the large, gold velvet curtains at the side of the screen.

'Now my dear, have you had enough yet?' the Jackal growled. He flicked back the curtain and there, in the corner of the room was a large, golden cage. Inside the cage, the Raven lay naked and curled up on the floor with a golden chain around her neck.

'How long do you have to stay in there before you are tame and won't fly away again?' he asked, 'Or do I need to remove one of your wings?' he laughed.

The Raven's long, black hair hung limply over her face and covered her expression, but the Meerkat and the Otter could hear her sobbing.

'We need to call the police M, this is crazy' the Otter whispered. The Otter and the Meerkat lay transfixed by the scene.

'We need to help her,' the Meerkat said. 'Maybe this is their thing?' the Otter whispered.

The Jackal was poking a large, metal rod into the cage and the Raven was making a high-pitched, shrill screeching sound.

'We need to go and get help, this is serious', the Meerkat said.

'Are you crazy?' the Otter replied. 'He'd skin us alive and happily keep our heads mounted on the wall in his study!' The Raven screeched again.

'Now!' the Meerkat said, and poked the Otter hard in the leg to snap him out of his trance.

They both crawled backwards, scared to make a sound. Then they scampered at full speed across the wet lawn towards the large fence at the back of the garden. The Otter, now running bare-footed, raced ahead of her. They both sprang over the fence, and as the Meerkat raced to the car, she turned to face the Otter.

'Where's your other shoe?' she said, seeing just one of his LV shoes in his hand.

He looked in disbelief at his hands. 'Fuck'. He slumped down in the grass panting and started crying.

Light suddenly flooded the garden and the Meerkat could hear a growling noise.

'Come on', the Meerkat shouted above the sound of the rain. 'We need to go and get help and I've got a plane to catch.'

Damn her inquisitive nature.

48 hours later --

Flying into Dharamshala, the Meerkat was amazed by the enormous sheet of rock stretching as high as the eye could see. The Himalayas. Dharamshala is the refuge home of the Tibetan people forced out from Tibet by the Chinese in 1970. She'd called the police anonymously from an old fashioned phone box outside the Jackal's house, amazed that it was still working, as it had been turned into a mini library, stacked high with books with a notice saying 'steal me'. The memory of the Raven kept filling her mind. She shook it free, it wasn't her problem.

Their small plane was just a tiny speck in the air, lost in the vastness of the mountains. That's how she felt: a small speck in the universe. Would her life mean anything to anyone?

The mountains were covered at the top in thick layers of snow, yet at the base, there was such a haze of intense heat that the tiny hilltop houses were just blocks of bright colour, blending into the green of the dense mountain trees. There was beauty and simplicity in the blending of the buildings and nature. The Tibetan people had made their home at the base of the mountain, crafting them into the rocks, then balancing them on enormous stilts that held these seemly fragile structures aloft.

When they arrived at the tiny village, it was filled with people selling from market stalls at the roadside. An abundance of hand-made objects crafted with immense skill. Necklaces carved from every natural material, hand woven scarves, knitted socks, animal skin hats and gloves – and much more. The Tibetan people that they were staying with welcomed them into their hotel with a warmth and gratitude that was overwhelming. They seemed so genuinely pleased to have them as guests that at night they ate with the whole Tibetan family. When they told them, they were visiting the Institute for an entire week they looked in amazement. The £125 they had paid for the week was three months' wages to them.

Two days before they visited the institute, they spent time climbing halfway up one of the mountains. They had set off early in the morning when it was dark and cold. The ice clung to the mountainside, making the way slippy and precarious. The Meerkat felt fear like she'd not experienced since she had been diagnosed with cancer. It followed her like a shadow. She was sure she was going to fall and die at any moment. Every step she took going up, she worried about the journey back down. Could she get back down? Would she slip on the ice when she descended? Her fear was so intense, she had to grapple with it to keep moving forward. Step by step, metre by metre. When they returned back down the mountain many hours later, the sun was out, and the ice had melted away, and she didn't have any problem with the descent. It showed her again that living in the future can be filled with fear. A fear that might never happen or be realised.

The next day, they visited the institute. The Indian government had granted the Tibetan monks a large piece of land at the base of the Himalayas in 1950. The institute was a mix of old and new buildings that kept springing up year on year, filled to the brim with smiling, laughing children of all ages dressed in the deep purple monks outfits with shaved heads. The local people sent their children to the school to be educated by the monks not just in Buddhism, but in French, English, science and maths. It was a great privilege to be accepted by the institute, as it held within its walls some of the most influential, learned Owls.

These Owls were not viewed as gods, but as extremely realised beings. To the Meerkat, they symbolised the wise men of old. Those who were placed among us to remind us of the basic ethics and morality of human life and goodness. They were mainly confined by the politics of their refugee status to remain just within India. Therefore, the light of their wisdom could only shine so far, and their circle of influence was small.

She wished they could share with her their insight with the world.

The Owl

From Creaturepedia, the distinctively homemade (but well researched :) encyclopaedia

Owls are mysterious, reclusive, nocturnal animals. Owls have at least two adaptations that aid them. First, the dull coloration of their feathers can render them almost invisible under certain conditions. Secondly, serrated edges on the own owls' wings muffle the sound of the flowing over the wing allowing an owls flight to be practically silent.

Description
Owls cannot move their eyes so have to move their whole head to look in any one direction. They have super sensitive hearing and their heads can swivel round in almost any direction as much as 270°.

Warning:
Owls symbolise wise and intelligent beings.

The Elephant and the Meerkat sat in a room with fifty other people of all different races, colours and origins. Tia Situ Ruma entered the room, a wise, ageing owl. Almost invisible, the Owl moved so silently, no one noticed him arrive.

'Please stand', his helpers commanded. The Meerkat stood up alert in surprise.

The Owl sat down on an ornate golden chair, his legs crossed, his face smiling. His head swivelled in every direction, gazing at this disparate group of creatures before him.

'At its heart', he said quietly, 'Buddhism is efficient. It's about doing things that foster serenity, happiness and confidence and avoiding things that provoke anxiety, fear and hopelessness. It's about recognising the inherent potential of your mind. Buddhism is not so concerned with getting you into good physical health. It's about recognising that you are here, right now, as a whole, as good, as essentially well as you could ever hope to be'. He paused.

'Buddhism training is not training like 'dog training', it's about helping you, guiding you to embody the Buddhist beliefs of kindness, consideration, compassion, joyfulness and ultimately to become Buddha. Buddha is a realised being that thinks not of the I, with fear, envy, competitiveness but of the whole of humanity with love, kindness and goodness. There are twelve things I want to teach you today', he concluded. 'I hope they will help you understand humanity more', he smiled.

The 12 teachings of the OWL.

1 **'Number One: Contamination.'** He paused. 'The mind is contaminated with rubbish. It's like a snowball of rubbish that we gather from the age of eight years old. We all have pureness in the middle (our middle), but we get overwhelmed with rubbish. The snowball picks up speed and size as we get older – the rubbish of greed, attachment, jealousy, competitiveness. We have got so caught up in the world's materialism and its definition of success (power and money), we have lost the basic virtues of being good to others and ourselves. If we thought less of the "I" and more of the good of the whole, the world would be a better place, with no jealousy, fear, suffering and ego.'

2 **'Number Two: Impermanence.'** We all have to first recognise that life is impermanent. Rich people, in their lifetime can grow poor. Good looking people can become ugly. Good health can turn quickly to lousy health, nothing is guaranteed. So, be prepared to die at any time. As soon as we are conceived, we are already on the path to death. Then when we are reborn and reincarnated as another sentient being, we could be your lunch, your mother, your father, or a being on another planet. If you were to die tomorrow, next week, or next month, or next year, would you live your life differently than you are doing today?' he questioned, looking at their eager faces. The Meerkat thought of the chicken sandwich and smiled: she'd not eaten one since.

3 **'Number Three: Being born human.'** It is special when we are born animals or human, many don't realise we are 'precious human life'. This in itself gives us qualities. In that, we were not born in hell, as a ghost. Human beings have an equal amount of suffering and happiness – being human is being compassion. If you had too much happiness, then why would you want to change? If you have too much suffering, you wouldn't be able

to see and evolve.'

4 **'Number Four: Suffering.'** Suffering is a path to realisation. Suffering is the broom which sweeps away the bad heart. To suffer in life is to be made more aware of its meaning. To experience life, everyone suffers. When you experience pain and sorrow you then know what true happiness is.

5 **'Number Five: Karma.'** What is in your mind? Is your intention good or bad? Are you happy if it's good or bad? How we think, feel, look, results in our karma. Karma is relative, not ultimate. Good karma can be destroyed by bad karma. Cause and condition. Karma isn't fate, Buddhahood is not karma. It is cause and effect. If we rejoice in others' suffering and pain and cause them pain, it's bad karma.'

The Meerkat thought of the Jackal and her cancer. The Jackal had brought cancer into the relationship. His behaviour was the cancer and he would never recover from what he'd
6 done, but maybe the Meerkat could.

'Number Six: Fear of dying or your loved ones dying.' You need to look death in the face, if you don't, it becomes a rock. If you look at it in the face, it becomes easy to break down and becomes more like shaving foam. We will all die, so you need to ensure you live a good life today.

7 **'Number Seven: Forgiveness.'** There is nothing that cannot be forgiven. Some people are full of arrogance and aggression that can't receive teachings, as they are full of pride and ego. There is not one crime you can't purify as long as you admit it. If you ignore it and don't take steps to change, it will eat at your soul.

8 **'Number Eight: Adversity.'** We all need to see a negative situation and use it as a path to learn and become enlightened. If creatures do harmful things to you, overcome them and

transform them. Learn from them and become wise.

9 **'Number Nine: Not liking yourself is wrong.'** When I visited the West, I was shocked. I could not have imagined that people didn't like themselves. I can't understand the West in that way. I love myself. I have compassion and kindness for myself. There are lots of black clouds, hail and wind that block the sunlight: we need to see the sun. So, stop focusing on the bad things and like ourselves and start doing good. If everyone saw themselves as one entity rather than single strands or pieces, we would all live more in harmony. Even if I break a million times, I will try a million times more.'

10 **'Number Ten: Ego is our biggest trouble maker.'** I am the ego. It limits you and causes you suffering. You need to be limitless. We believe that if we achieve our desires, we will be happy, but success isn't happiness. We, humans, are always running around in circles like ants, days and nights just to get what we want. All because of "I" – if you could be there in your own mind, it would be "me, me, me, me". But intelligent life is impermanent, you wouldn't waste any time. Self-esteem should be like space, not like a big meatloaf: limitless.

11 **'Number Eleven: Bad health.'** Wishing it hadn't happened to you: "why me?" means that it should have happened to someone else.

12 **Number Twelve: Be prepared to die at anytime.'** Imagine you are a baby with a blindfold that is pushed off a large mountain; you know you will hit the floor, but you are not sure if it's tomorrow, ten years away, or a whole lifetime. When you have an illness, the blindfold comes off and you see the floor. With this realisation, you are aware of your end.'

'The world will be saved by the western woman'

Dalai Lama

On their final day, they went for their appointment with the Owl. He lived in a house that stood at the side of the village, not overpowering or princely, but underwhelming and straightforward. A powerful peacefulness echoed within its corridors as they arrived. Fifty creatures in small groups waited in silence. Males in ancient Indian robes, tourists from South Africa, a group of children in monk's outfits, a wealthy banker and his wife. As each group was introduced to the Owl, he held their hands and listened intently to their questions and stories with love in his eyes.

The Meerkat and the Elephant were the last to see him. He walked over to them slowly, his eighty-six years showing in his movements, but not on his face. He reached out and held the Meerkat's right hand, and he never let it go the whole ten minutes they talked. The warmth of his hand crept up through her body and warmed her heart.

'What can I do to help the world?' the Meerkat asked.

'That is a huge question for such a small amount of time,' he said and smiled. Yet, time seemed to stand still. There was no rush or sign of impatience from him.

'The world will be saved by the western woman,' he said softly. 'Some people may call me a feminist, but we need more effort to promote basic human values – human compassion, human affection. And in that respect, most females have more sensitivity for others' pain and suffering'.

The Meerkat and the Elephant remained silent, intensely listening.

'Through healing ourselves, we create a vibrational shift', he said. 'Through healing ourselves we are able to be better friends, lovers, partners, colleagues, mothers and wives. Through healing ourselves, we will also heal the planet. Through aligning our lives, we will effortlessly light up the world with our unique presence. We each have an inner light that is always waiting to guide us home', he paused.

'When we allow this light to lead us and when we share that light with the world, we fall into flow with the universe. When we fall into flow with the universe, we are living the life that we are most called to live', he paused and softly squeezed her right hand. 'Are you doing this?' he asked them. They both frowned.

'We all', he whispered, 'need to move on from the suffering and start living again, with life we can do great good.'

The Owl handed them both as a final kind gesture, a red cord. The Meerkat had read that these cords could bring good luck or offer some kind of protection. In the traditional practice, the Owl tied a knot in the cable, blew a mantra into it and made a blessing. Many years later, the real significance of the red cord presented its meaning to the Meerkat. She only became aware of its importance when she was asked to take it off. She had taken the Baby Bear to the Go Ape climbing school.

'You can't go up there with that on', the climbing instructor said, as he jabbed at the red cord on her wrist.

To say she just had a panic attack was underplaying the event. The red cord had come to signify her survival. If she took it off her wrist, she thought, she would die. The Owl had never said that

'Chaining an elephant isn't as simple as just putting a chain around its leg – an adult elephant could snap that chain without even noticing the effort. The way to chain an elephant is to start when it's a baby. You don't even need a chain – a strong rope will do. The baby elephant will struggle, but eventually, it will realise that it can't break the cable, and even worse, continuing to fight creates a painful burn on its leg. The baby elephant learns not to struggle – it accepts that the limit imposed by the rope or chain is permanent, and there is no use fighting against it. Sure, the elephant grows up and becomes the most powerful land mammal on the face of the earth. But the chains in its mind remains strong, and so the chains on its leg are never broken.'

The relief that came with the thought that I could with one lift of my foot cut the shackles of the past was incredible. "But how?", I asked the Owl.' Ele said.

'It's in your hands to transform your pain into victory", he said. *"Transform your pain of abuse into strength to defend the woman who cannot speak up."* M, he's given me a place in the institute helping young abused women'. She smiled a sad smile.

'I think I've found my calling, no more searching for me; I start next month, I'm just coming back to collect my things, and to see that the Jackal pays, I'm going to the police to make a report'.

'Have patience with all things, but chiefly, have patience with yourself. Do not lose courage by considering your own imperfections, but instantly set about remedying them: every day, begin the task anew.'

Francis de Sales

As they landed at Heathrow, the polished modernity of the airport took the Meerkat by surprise: a stark contrast to the earthiness of India. She'd been there hundreds of times before, but somehow things had changed. Everything had changed. Vivid images of her time in India floated around in her mind: how long had she been gone? She felt nothing but confusion and lightheadedness. It must be the shock of the confession.

As she disembarked from the plane, her head started spinning, and her arm began to ache and throb. In a daze, she rolled up her sleeve: a bright red rash had appeared. She itched at it furiously, trying to rub it away. By the time she had gone through passport control, she could feel the outbreak spreading, her neck prickled and throbbed in pain. By the time she had seen her rucksack on the conveyor belt, she felt so sick, she struggled to stand. Her fingers brushed over her rucksack's strap as it moved past her. She didn't have the strength to grab it. Slowly taking all her belongings with it, it disappeared. She could feel the sweat dripping down her forehead and a voice talking to her from afar.

'M, are you ok?', the Elephant asked with concern.

The last thing she remembered was slipping down into the darkness.

When she woke, she was lying down. Her body ached – every millimetre of it. A dull, roaring pain. She opened her eyes. She would have gone back to sleep, but the ache that held her body tight turned to pain. She was thirsty. She felt that she had been thirsty for a very long time.

'Water' – her voice, cracked and weak, sounded remote to her.

'Water', she asked again in a voice that she didn't recognise.

A cup of water was placed next to her dry mouth.

'What's wrong with me?' she whispered.

'Ssh', the voice said in a low growl.

Her mind slipped in and out of consciousness like she was somehow two entities, neither she could hold on to.

Nothing seemed real. She tried to remember her name. From the depths of her mind, she heard a hard slamming sound and a gush of air against her face. Slamming the door hard against the wall, the Jackal confidently strode into the room. She could smell his anger and rage.

'I'VE LOST EVERYTHING'

his voice screamed

She tried to open her eyes.

He suddenly stopped. He looked up and down, soaking in the surroundings, the smells, the texture. His look of anger turned into fear. Fear entered his eyes and paused his sentence in mid-flow. A sense of worry, disbelief and frustration took the bitter chill from his voice, and he whispered.

'Do you think I'm sorry about the Elephant, that's why I'm here?' He paused and cocked his head to one side, waiting.

Silence.

'That bitch has made up a pack of lies and told them to the police', he said, challenging the Meerkat. Daring her to answer. Imploring her with his exhausted, bloodshot eyes.

'And what the hell were you doing in my garden?' He threw the LV shoe hard against the wall. 'Was it you who called the fucking police? I was in that shit hole all night, answering question after fucking question.'

The Jackal's questions were left hanging in the air, unanswered and unexplored. She could see from the corner of her eye the Bear sitting quietly in the corner of the room. The Jackal paced over to the bed and started stroking her hair.

'Go away', the Meerkat whispered.

The Jackal blinked with shock and smiled sadly.

'You look just like her', he said. 'Do you think you will die?', he asked.

'Who?' asked the Meerkat; she felt fear in her heart.

'Your sister, you look just like your sister. She was a near perfect image of you', he sneered. 'Oh, how you wronged me. Imagine how hurt I was to find out about you and the Bear, behind my back when we were first together. Both of you laughing at me. Then you just left – no sorry or real explanation. I was drunk all the time when you left. She was cycling. I was drunk. Driving my car. She smiled when she saw me in the car. Oh, how like you, just more perfect, more fine-tuned. Then she swerved and fell off her bike onto the road. I tried to swerve, but I hit her. I couldn't stop to see how she was you know, I was drunk, and it would have ruined my life. I need to set the record straight so this stops haunting me.'

He started to cry into his hands. 'I love you M, please forgive me.'

The Bear growled, then moved quickly and quietly to the Jackal's side and yanked him back by his shoulders.

'GO AWAY, YOU ARE NOT WANTED HERE. SHE HATES YOU, YOU BASTARD!' he yelled at the Jackal.

The forcefulness of his words was as impactful as if he'd visibly punched him. The Jackal jumped back, shocked and startled. He then suddenly threw himself at the Bear. Losing all control. Laying into the Bear's chest with real punches, clawing and spitting into his face.

'IT'S ALL YOUR FAULT', the Jackal screamed at the Bear. **'SHE'S MINE'.**

As the Bear lay bleeding on the floor, the Jackal stopped and stood to pant, his smooth, perfect hair all dishevelled and his eyes frantic with panic.

'I hate you', the Meerkat whispered to the Jackal.

'But I can't live without you', the Jackal cried.

The Meerkat paused, looked him directly in the eye and whispered with pure hate in her eyes, 'Then why aren't you dead yet?' The Jackal blanched.

A cold breeze blew in through the half-opened window, bringing an acute chill to the air. She shivered. Two hands violently grabbed at her neck and shook her. She could feel droplets of spit hit her violently in the face as he laughed. A stale breath filled her lungs as she blacked out into unconsciousness and thought of her sister.

The Meerkat. Emily. Em, as everyone called her, was standing in the wooden house: the miniature version of her own childhood home, the one perfectly made by her father for her and her sister for Christmas. Frozen in time. Its façade was painted white, with a clay-tiled roof, which was green with moss. Its dormer windows made it look like it was smiling, even from the outside. Her parents had an eclectic taste. Its hand-drawn wallpaper, with images of Jackals chasing mad Meerkats, pressed carefully against hand crafted furniture. A stuffed Otter with scrabbling paws, a Raven and a Robin were arranged on their antique dresser, frozen in time, their black eyes dead. A small, bronze lamp crafted into the shape of a Fox and a Fawn hand in hand created a glow in the room, and the smell of baking filled the air with a sweet scent.

Em, her mum, her dad and her sister Joanna – the perfectly contented four. They were all in the kitchen . Em's mother was singing a song as she weighed out the ingredients for a cake, while her dad sat humming a tune on an old, grey trunk covered with elephant stickers from their trip to India. Em and her sister were adding lavender and vanilla into a bowl and taking it in turn to stir the mixture. Her big, soft, brown Bear, teddy sat watching, she carried him everywhere. Smiles and laughter fill the room. Her mother looked on with love at her two almost-identical daughters and smiled a knowing smile that only mothers can have.

'You girls will be famous bakers when you grow up, you've both got such natural talent, don't you think father?' her mother laughed and started singing a silly song and her father laughed along to its rhythm. Em smiled and watched her family – how much love in one room. She stroked the small Chameleon brooch given to her by her sister for Christmas the year before, its skin changed colour depending on the light in the room.

'Famous bakers', her mother smiled again. 'For sure', her father said and hugged both the girls in one big embrace till they squealed in delight.

'You two will be stars', he smiled.

When the Meerkat regained consciousness, the perfect dream faded. She sobbed into the Bear's arms and longed for the life that her sister Jo was never allowed to live. He'd wrenched his brother's hands from her neck and sobbed too.

When the Bear thought the Meerkat had started to look more herself, he handed her a folded-up newspaper. The Bear's battered blue face never smiled or was smug, just calm and resigned as he placed it carefully into her hand. She never read real newspapers anymore, its texture felt unnatural in her hand. She turned it over and opened up the folded pages, he'd highlighted a story on the front cover which immediately caught her attention. It now all made sense. They had arrested the Jackal and had led him away, no one knew what had happened.

Devour files for Administration, Devour CEO the Bull arrested for client data abuse.

By: Angela Fortnight, the Daily News.

The restaurant group Devour was dealt a blow today when it went into administration. The Bull, the company's Chairman and board director was discovered to be selling customer information to the rival restaurant group EVE. Today's update induced the ICO intention to fine Devour 5 million pounds. The probe concluded that Devour had contravened the law by failing to safeguard people's information. It also found that the company failed to be transparent about how people's data was harvested by others.

EVE CEO is arrested for rape and hit and run murder.

By: Angela Fortnight, the Daily News

Police have arrested the CEO of EVE, the Jackal, following an accusation of data harvesting, rape and a hit and run murder committed ten years previously. He will stand trial in London on the 4th September.

'I'm an innocent man', he stated when questioned by reporters outside of the court. 'Clearly, someone is out to get me and I'm adamant that I will clear my good name.'

A photo of the Jackal hand in hand with the Raven filled the front page.

At this stage, police won't comment further until a full investigation is conducted. His wife is standing by him.

'This is slander', she was quoted as saying. 'We won't rest until our lawyers have brought these individuals who are slandering our good name to court.'

Her multimillion-pound property developer father was funding the legal case.

'When you think everything is someone else's fault, you will suffer a lot. When you realise that everything springs from yourself, you will learn both peace and joy.'

Dalai Lama

'The ignorant are ignorant of their ignorance.'

Peter Baskerville.

Timidly, they approached the church. The police had finally released the Chameleon's body.

'How could I possibly not go?' the Meerkat said to the Elephant and Bear's disbelieving faces earlier that day in the hospital. 'She'd never forgive me, I owe her this much.' Her cheeks had sunk into her face, her arm hung limply at her side and her skin had gone a pale, soft, snowy-white. Red, angry finger marks surrounded her neck.

They sat in the back visitation room, a place of exposed stone off to the side of the sanctuary to the Catholic church of St Mary's. There were maybe a hundred chairs set up in the room, and it was three-quarters full, but felt a quarter empty. The church was filled with colourful, crying, keening creatures. It felt strangely overplayed to the Meerkat, like a West-End musical where everyone sings loudly and gestures wildly. Big, overplayed movements, dramatic scenes and overblown emotions. For a while, she just watched, as individuals walked up to the coffin, which was on some kind of table with a navy and gold tablecloth. Individuals she'd never seen before would stand over the Chameleon and look for a while, maybe say something, cry a little or touch her chest. All left with tears in their eyes.

'Where has the Chameleon gone?' she whispered to the Elephant. 'All that life, that energy, that love, gone?'

The Elephant smiled. 'Not gone, she's here now, all ready to start her life again.'

The Chameleon's parents were standing next to the coffin, hugging everyone as they passed by. When they noticed the Meerkat, they frowned. The Meerkat just couldn't help but think that now the Chameleon had gone, the embarrassment of having a transsexual son would be hidden away. His parents could go back to their old lives, where their neighbours didn't smirk every time the Chameleon, in her latest elaborate, feminine outfit, would walk up into their house. They could now concentrate all their hopes on his other siblings.

'...A grandchild quite soon', the Meerkat had overheard the Chameleon's mother saying earlier to her sister. 'A handsome son-in-law, my eldest daughter's probably hiding him in the background, you know how secretive she can be', she had glowed with the thought of it. 'She's the eldest, it's got to happen soon' she sighed.

The Meerkat walked over to the open coffin. She knew it would be like looking at a hollow shell. When she looked into the coffin, the Chameleon was dressed like a man she didn't know. A stiff navy-blue suit, a crisp white shirt and a tie. Her hair had been cut short and was parted neatly on the left side in a way that she would have found absolutely horrifying.

Once she had got over the shock of the Chameleon's parents' final betrayal, she stood there looking at her and wondering when some feeling would hit her. But oddly there was a blankness of thought. There was nothing more she could do, but what she wanted to do was shake her by the shoulders, put some life into her. She had once loved her so much: it was a silly thought, she knew. Like banging the side of a TV, it was such a strong urge, but the moment went.

'It's okay, Cam. It's okay. It is. It's okay. I'm sorry, I wish I'd listened harder and heard you more. I wish I'd have given you more time and understood the depths of despair you were feeling. It's okay.' the Meerkat said into the coffin.

She snapped open her bag, reached in and pulled out a red silk scarf with tiny green flowers embroidered into its fabric and gently placed it around the Chameleon's neck. The memory, so crisp and clear in her mind, of one of their first dates in Harrods when he played the piano for her. How had she not known then?

'He loved you too much,' the Chameleon's mother said over her shoulder. 'You ruined his life and turned him into someone he was not'. The spit from her mouth hit the Meerkat in the face, she wiped her face with the back of her hand and returned to the back of the church.

The minister stood up and walked to the coffin. He described how brave the Chameleon had been, how much loved ***HE*** was, how inspirational ***HE*** was. The Chameleon's parents nodded in approval at his every word. When he'd finished his speech, the Minister invited the Chameleon's sister up to the pulpit. The Chameleon's sister stood up, looking the Meerkat straight in the eye. She paused and then began her carefully written eulogy to her sibling.

'When I was five, ***SHE*** would patiently teach me to play the piano. ***SHE*** would hold my hand in the night when I was scared of the dark, but more importantly, ***SHE*** would tell me that I was the best sister life could give and that ***SHE*** was so deeply proud of me. I found in her a braveness and determination to stand up for what ***SHE*** believed in that I envied'. She paused. 'A thirst to drive a new path for people like her, however difficult ***SHE*** knew that would be. I'm so proud to call her my friend and my sister, a friend who lived every day being as true to herself as anyone could be. ***SHE*** alone has given me the determination to be the real, true me.'

With that, she walked off the pulpit and into the arms of her Brazilian lesbian lover, kissing her passionately on the lips. Most of the congregation roared and clapped with approval, except for the Chameleon's parents and the church minister. With cross faces, they turned their shaking heads away.

Ignorance is sometimes bliss, when you can't handle the truth of a situation.

The Crab took the empty seat in the church beside her and tentatively reached for the Meerkat's hand. The Meerkat looked at the Elephant who just nodded, her face blank. The Meerkat turned around, looked the Crab straight in the eye, smiled and held her hand tightly. Too much loss, too much regret.

'I've lost everything', the Crab said to the Meerkat.

'Everything?' The Meerkat queried with surprised eyes.

'Yes, he's cleared out all of our bank accounts, quietly sold our houses, sold all the cars, the boat – and more, and just went. Her eyes glistened with tears. 'Ironically, he was the one, the one that I loved the most of them all', the Crab said.

'I'm so sorry', said the Meerkat. For all of their loss. The business. Their friendship. Their love.

'He just left me with one, tiny thing', the Crab sighed and looked down at her stomach and smiled a sad smile. A small growing mound appeared under her dress.

'Oh C, I'm so happy for you, not everything,' said the Meerkat. 'Now you can really start living again, he left you the most important gift in your life, you will see', she smiled.

The church was strangely silent. The coffin looked all alone. She wished that she could comfort Cam and talk to her again. How much she wanted to say, so many things left that would never be said.

'M, there is something I came to tell you,' the Crab sighed. 'I'm sorry it has to be me', she said, looking down at her feet.

'What is it?', the Meerkat whispered, afraid of what she would say next.

'There is one thing the Bull told me before he left, a final parting comment'. The Crab started sobbing into her hands.

'He said that the Chameleon's death wasn't suicide.' The Crab paused. 'He said that it was the Jackal's final act of revenge on you.'

'Revenge?', the Meerkat stuttered.

'The Bear's untouchable, he always was,' she sighed. 'Weirdly, I think he loves him as much as you. But he knew you loved the Chameleon and she was close to the edge, so he just took the opportunity to push.'

The day THE CHAMELEON left the earth for good --------

The Jackal knocked on the door of the Chameleon's run down co-operative house. As his hard, swift knock vibrated the door, red paint flaked off and dropped to the floor. He peered into one of the small, stained glass windows but they were so thick with dirt and dust he couldn't see in. He quickly brushed his black leather gloves clean. Disgusting. Seething, he waited. The house was dark and quiet, the housemates of the Chameleon were out for the night. The Jackal had made sure of that. Free tickets to EVE he'd posted only the day before. The door swung open, and the Chameleon in his favourite butterfly dress stood proud and animated on the step.

'Hello, my love', the Chameleon said to the Jackal and stroked his handsome face. The Jackal tried hard not to recoil.

'I need a new act for my club', the Jackal had said to the Chameleon a few months before. The Chameleon, forlorn and rejected, was sitting in the cheap cafe with a 40p cup of trucker tea in a pink fur coat and high-heeled pink shoes, crying.

'I hear you can play the piano and can sing?' the Jackal continued, ignoring the tears. 'A bit', the Chameleon sniffed, 'but I'm not very good,' she sighed. ' I'm not very good at anything'

'You are exactly what I need in my club, Eve,' the Jackal said. 'Exactly – I can make you famous young lady'.

The Chameleon looked with a curious gaze and smiled at this extraordinarily handsome male. She'd left the Meerkat on the Southbank only an hour before. The memories of her smell and their ride on the carousel filled her mind with a happiness she knew she could never have again. The Meerkat was in love with the Bear and always had been. Had she ever loved her? The Chameleon wasn't sure anymore.

'Do I know you?', the Chameleon frowned.

'Not yet', the Jackal said. 'but we have lots in common.' He smiled his most handsome smile and the Chameleon blushed.

At the Funeral --

The service came to an end, and the sobbing crowd were ushered to the main doors and out into the graveyard covered with dark and stormy clouds. The Meerkat didn't want to see the Chameleon lowered into the ground, or her lover fall to his feet sobbing. She didn't want to see the Chameleon's Colourful friends singing their last song to her with all of their love. But she did.

The day THE CHAMELEON left the earth for good--------

'Hello, my love', the Chameleon said to the Jackal again. She watched the Jackal recoil. She watched him clench his fist. The Chameleon had gone too far that night at EVE.

'My last song', the Chameleon had said, 'is dedicated to my one and only true love and soulmate the Meerkat; how much I love her.' She smiled tenderly into the crowd, 'I've written this final song, especially for her.'

The Jackal had stopped drinking and laughing with his pack and looked over at the Chameleon poised ready to play and scowled. The Raven sitting next to him winced. She was painfully thin and painfully sad. She laughed a pinched laugh every time the Jackal laughed. Her son was all she had and he'd promised her she'd never see him again if she left again. She believed him. A week in the cage had taught her what depravities he could inflict on another. The new diamond rings, necklaces and bracelets he'd bought her recently felt like hollow stones adorning her light, feathery skin.

'The Meerkat. My Emily. My Em is beautiful inside and out. She's mischievous and captivating', a tear ran down the Chameleon's face, 'and today my friends, is her birthday,' she smiled a tender smile, 'and I have the best present ever.' The Chameleon felt the memory stick in her pocket. 'The Meerkat captured all of our hearts – some softly in the night and some with a tight, grasping hold.' The Eve waitresses and bar staff smiled and nodded.

The Chameleon looked over at the Jackal and frowned. She knew. She knew about them. She also knew that the Jackal had raped the Elephant and she knew about the Meerkat's sister. Little hints and brags here and there, little clues and the lengths he would go to for revenge, she knew. Piece by piece her intelligent, fast-thinking brain had discovered the truth and when she'd confronted the Jackal that afternoon, he'd admitted it all bit by bit, even gloating over all the details.

'The Meerkat's sister, what a waste, such a beautiful creature, too beautiful for road kill,' the Jackal had said it almost with sadness – or was he just mirroring the Chameleon's anguished, expressions? Devastated, the Chameleon kept up the charade. The Chameleon had recorded the full confession. She had the memory stick in her butterfly pocket ready to give to the Meerkat after her last ever song at EVE. The Jackal had made her famous as he'd promised, her songs were being played in all the London clubs and she'd even heard on the radio this morning. None of it made her happy. She was going to tell the Jackal in the morning she was leaving.

The Chameleon smiled at the Jackal as he prowled cautiously into her house. 'Everything ok, my love?' she asked. The Jackal nodded. He walked slowly with his ears pricked, like he was searching for prey. He trailed her slowly and watched her disappear into the lounge, looking for one of her many flatmates – they were always there. She froze in the doorway. The Jackal entered the lounge. Hundreds of dead eyes watched him. The Chameleon's taxidermy obsession had gotten out of control since she'd left the Meerkat. Tiny birds, rabbits, badgers, insects and butterflies filled the room.

'One should never be too smart or too cunning', the Jackal smiled. 'Especially around a Jackal. No one here?', the Jackal asked. Perfectly aware from his manager that all the Chameleon's flatmates were currently downing free drinks and food in the club – the scavengers.

The Jackal's eyes flicked around the room and settled on a brown, hessian cable connected to a red hammock lying on the floor.

'Now, there is something I need you to write for me', he pulled out a piece of white paper and an old Biro from his pocket and handed it to the surprised Chameleon.

'Don't worry, I have an old version I found in your changing room, this has obviously been on your mind for a while, so consider this as a favour.' The Jackal handed the Chameleon a letter penned in her own hand. A suicide note.

'Oh, and there is something you have of mine that I need,' he said. 'A memorystick perhaps?' The Chameleon instinctively reached inside her pocket and clutched at the stick. 'I made a silly mistake of letting my wife find one of those things before and I won't be doing that again in a hurry', he smiled.

The Jackal spread out his jacket on the sofa, lay down and waited for the Chameleon to finish the letter. The Chameleon's quick brain was playing for time. The Jackal shut his eyes. She finished the letter and then slowly and carefully grabbed a stuffed rabbit with a heavy metal base from the shelf. She then Rabbit punched the Jackal in the head. Thump. Thump. Thump.

The Jackal lay very still, very dead.

The house grew silent. The Chameleon collapsed onto the floor. It was over. All the stuffed animals applauded.

With lightning speed, the Jackal jumped up and reached for the cable and the red hammock cloth flapped to the floor. His hands twisted it into a firm knot and he held it close to the Chameleon's face as her skin turned a snowy, pale grey.

A waft of lavender from the red hammock filled the air. The same red hammock that it felt like only minutes before she had so happily folded into the delicate shape of the Meerkat as they lay next to each other in their dream garden. The Chameleon was so happy then.

As she died seconds later, the Chameleon's last thought was of only one thing – her true love, the Meerkat. Resigned, the thought added a tiny comfort to her panicking mind – then she was free.

At the funeral --

The Crab threw her wedding ring into the grave as they walked away; it hit the wood of the coffin with a dull thump. A tear slipped down from her eye and she brushed it away. 'I'm sorry, E' she whispered. The Meerkat watched for a reaction. The Elephant continued walking forward without any change of expression. *It's strange,* thought the Meerkat, watching her actions, h*ow much pain we can bring on ourselves*. We are all looking for answers, we all want to make sure we live our lives well. Sometimes just saying the word 'sorry' simply isn't enough.

The Meerkat felt the warmth of the sun on her face as it came from behind the dark clouds, and she suddenly found a calmness.

Epilogue

'Hold on', the Meerkat said, as she held back from the group.

As she looked over at the entrance to the graveyard, the Jackal quickly disappeared behind a tree. She called the police and watched them escort him away, fighting. A small, beautiful butterfly landed on her shoulder close to her ear. Red with green flecks: such an unusual, delicate, colourful creature she thought. She watched its flickering wings, its minor perturbations, its tiny antennae twitching back and forth like it was listening for something, or someone.

She'd been told days earlier by the Owl to watch for it; she hadn't quite understood then.

'Out of the sadness will come such freedom and beauty,' he'd said. 'Small changes in life can create a significant outcome: forecasting the future can be nearly impossible', he said. 'But, no one is ever gone, death is only a doorway to a new life', he smiled.

She watched the butterfly take off into the cool summer air.

'Be free', she whispered into the air.

The butterfly was finally free, for two whole weeks, to live on the earth as it chose. Wild and free within nature. Proud of its true self. Free from judgment, a thing of beauty that everyone could adore and love. A special gift of the circle of life.

What next? thought the Meerkat, as she walked back to her endlessly patient Bear, smiling, the memory of the butterfly's whispers crisp in her mind.

'I'm finally free my love, no more pain.'

'Don't Count the Days; Make the Days Count.'

The Soul of a Butterfly: Reflections on Life's Journey

Muhammad Ali

Please share your experience:

If you have enjoyed this novel please share your experience with us. All feedback will be included into the final version before it goes to publish in 2020.

Email: Julia.leckey@icloud.com
Instagram: @JuliaLeckeyAuthor, @emmaetrose
Twitter: JuliaLeckeyAuthor@JuliaLeckey1, @emmaetrose
Website: www.colourful-creatures.com

COLOURFUL CREATURES
COLOURFUL CREATURES
COLOURFUL CREATURES
COLOURFUL CREATURES
COLOURFUL CREATURES
COLOURFUL CREATURES